I0551325

# Falling in Love

# Despite

# Christmas Miscalculations

Christine L Henderson

*"I love you not only for what you are, but for what I am when I am with you. I love you not only for what you have made of yourself, but for what you are making of me. I love you for the part of me that you bring out."*

Elizabeth Barrett Browning

1

Copyright 2025  Christine L. Henderson
**Falling in Love Despite Christmas Miscalculations**
**Christine L. Henderson**
**ISBN: 979-8-9986150-1-6**

www.christinelhenderson.com

All rights reserved. This book or parts thereof may not be reproduced in any form, stored in any retrieval system, or transmitted in any form by any means—electronic, mechanical, photocopy, recording, or otherwise—without prior written permission of the publisher, except as provided by United States of America copyright law and fair use.

This is a work of fiction. Names, characters, businesses, places, events, locales, and incidents are either the products of the author's imagination or used in a fictitious manner. Any resemblance to actual persons, living or dead, or actual events is purely coincidental.

*I appreciate the time you spent reading this story and hope you liked it as much as I enjoyed creating these characters and storyline. I would be especially grateful if you would consider leaving a review wherever you purchase your books. Thank you.*

# Chapter 1

## Natalie

Natalie Baynton pushed her luggage into the elevator at the Snowmass hotel for Rothwell's employees. She closed her eyes for a moment and exhaled a deep breath. As the elevator ascended to the fourth floor, so did her hopes for tomorrow. The mini suite she'd be sharing with her new roommate awaited her. This new job was a significant step towards the future she had long envisioned.

Staring blankly ahead, her mind raced with thoughts of tomorrow. This job wasn't just employment—it was a golden ticket to her ultimate goal of becoming a fashion buyer. For a decade, she had balanced full-time work with the relentless pursuit of her undergraduate and master's degrees in fashion marketing, sacrificing countless nights and weekends for a shot at her dream.

Her last boyfriend had scoffed at her fashion ambitions, dismissing her higher education pursuits as a frivolous expense when, in his mind, she could simply climb the ranks at a local upscale department store. His only interest seemed to be the benefits he could reap from her store discount, flaunting his new wardrobe while wining and dining another woman behind her back. Discovering his betrayal had been painful, but it made her even more focused on her career. Now with a determined heart, she was ready to prove that her dreams were worth every sacrifice.

The recommendations from instructors and past small retail employers got her this job. Now she would need to prove worthy of continuing to work in the fashion marketing department beyond her four month paid internship position. Their Aspen location opened a year ago and it was already considered one of the hot spots for the rich with its extravagant upscale clothing line for daytime, playtime, and night time chic. Though she lived in Colorado all her life, this was her first visit to Aspen, and she hoped it would become her permanent home.

She'd read everything she could about their first location at St. Moritz, Switzerland and was in awe of the store's design layout and couldn't wait to see and touch the luxury lines of clothing. Although her meager salary and provided living arrangements would hardly give her the funds to buy anything there, she'd enjoy setting up the displays and dressing the mannequins pretending they were her own clothes.

As she stopped at the assigned door number, she hesitated. Would she get along with her new roommate? Rothwell's set up the pairings of employees, but they had never met. The job acceptance letter gave some details of Laura Farnaby's academic and work history, but would their personalities mesh? She tapped on the door and heard a cheery voice say, "Just a minute."

When the door opened, Natalie was greeted by a smiling female with a perfectly sculpted face whose long blonde hair was twirled in a bun, Her slim figure displayed a

Northern Colorado Nightmare football team sweatshirt, jeans, and socks.

Before she could say the word, Laura gushed, "You must be my new roommate Natalie. Come on in. I've just been here a couple hours myself and killing time until you got here so we could make plans on how to share our mini suite."

In her best Vanna White impression with full style and flair, she began to walk through their living space. "It has everything we need… living room with a non-descript sofa, dining nook and mini kitchen all in one… but there are two TVs, one in this room and the bedroom, which we'll share. However, the room does have lots of storage even though we don't really need much space as we'll be wearing Rothwell's uniforms…"

Natalie smiled at Laura's enthusiasm. Although she had only been there a couple of hours, she had already unpacked her clothes, placed favorite pictures on her dresser, added coffee mugs of her football team by the coffee machine and made it feel like home.

Laura's tour ended in the bedroom where she sat cross-legged on her bed and directed Natalie to unpack.

"What do you want to do next after unpacking? I think we should check out the cafeteria and then find our way over to Rothwell's so we'll know how long it will take to get to the store for our orientation tomorrow. Roaring Fork Transit, or RFTA, has a stop right in front of our building and a stop at the store, which is very convenient. Is your orientation at 7:00 AM like mine?"

Natalie stopped her unpacking and began reciting the next day's schedule, counting them on her fingers. "Yes. I memorized the details. The main orientation will take one hour. Then we break into department groups for another 30 minutes. Then go to the store, familiarize ourselves as to where items are located if guests ask us questions. All before the store opens. Next, we split into groups again –"

"Wow, Natalie. You are truly detail oriented. Anytime I have any questions about work, I'll know who to ask."

Natalie shrugged and returned to unpacking. "This job is important to me. I've been working in retail since high school. Since then, I've received my undergrad and graduate degrees in Apparel and Merchandising. This is my passion. My chance to become their fashion buyer."

"I love fashion, but you're way more focused. I've been doing modeling jobs for car shows, video tours for area home developers, and local TV ads. I want something more permanent, not just short term. I signed up for Rothwell's main fashion shows, but I'll also do their pop-up shows and videos."

Perplexed, Natalie replied, "Pop-up shows?"

"Yes, it's a Rothwell's exclusive." Laura's eyes lit up and she became animated. "It's fun to do. Each department has a pop out cat walk. When the mini show begins, the cat walk is extended. Music and strobe lights focus on the models. We do our walk, then hand out marketing sheets showing how to buy the complete ensemble. Those shows are put up as scrolling videos afterwards in the department for more interest."

"Good marketing technique. There's more impact for potential buyers in seeing clothes on a model rather than on a lifeless mannequin -- even if the shopper isn't a model perfect size."

Laura continued talking as she stepped to the kitchenette to get a bottle of water. "I love modeling but hate having to watch every single bite of food to make sure I can fit into those slim and sleek clothes. I really want something more than being a model."

"Maybe you could become the "face" of a luxury brand. Like Charlize Theron for J'Adore. Keira Knightley for Chanel, or Zendaya for Bulgari."

"I'd like that. Or maybe wearing those elegant designer outfits, I'll catch the attention of a good looking rich guy, who doesn't care if I gain a few pounds. We'll run off to his chateau and live happily ever after."

"You really think that will happen?" Natalie smirked. "You'll be better off if you get that chateau on your own rather than waiting for Prince Charming to appear."

Laura laughed. "Hey, a girl can dream. I'll be happy if I can go on dates with guys who bring me flowers or maybe dazzle me with gifts from Rothwell's."

"Nope. Not me. Done with dating. I don't need that drama again." She closed the last drawer and turned toward Laura. "My career is my focus. Not looking for Mr. Perfectly Right or even Mr. Almost Right."

"Hope you'll make *some* time for fun." Laura rolled her eyes. "As the saying goes, all work and no play makes

Natalie a very lonely and depressed girl. C'mon let scope out the building's cafeteria. They're supposed to have a fantastic coffee machine that can make coffee, espresso, latte, hot cocoa, and tea."

"Great idea. Can't wait to see the store tomorrow. Lord willing it'll be the start of something great for both of us.

# Chapter 2

## Alexander

Emma gave a final touch up to her lipstick, then glared at her brother. "Alexander, stop whatever you're doing with your phone. You promised to take me to Rothwell's. I'm ready now."

Alexander rolled his eyes. "About time. You said you'd be ready an hour ago. If you weren't my sister, I would have left you here." As he turned to face her, he raised his hands. "I'm supposed to keep a low profile. You look like you're headed to some designer fashion show and trying to catch the eye of the paparazzi."

"Yes, I do look fabulous. But I'm not the one who needs to keep a low profile. I'm here on vacation." Emma put a hand on Alexander's shoulder as she held up a Rothwell's shopping bag in her other one. "Act as my personal shopper. Take this scarf to the returns department. That way you can review whoever works there.

While you evaluate other staffers incognito, I'll shop. You do look rather average in your sweater and designer jeans, but you should tousle your hair a bit so it's not perfectly coiffed."

"Right." He raked his fingers through his hair, then tossed his head back. "How's that?"

"Much better. You look less than your normal smart self. Now don't forget to bow to me as I send you off to do my bidding."

Alexander clapped his hands together and laughed. "Oh I can see you're going to have a fun time with this, aren't you, dear sister."

"Yes it'll be like when we were children, and we performed our little plays for Mummy and Daddy."

"Only try not to be quite so dramatic. We're not performing Shakespeare."

"I'll do my best to not overplay my part. Now, let's go. I have lunch planned with a new friend and I don't want to be late."

When they entered the store, Alexander let Emma lead a step or two ahead while he held her petite shopping bag and a notepad in his hand. They played their little charade and Alexander left to find the returns department. When he arrived there, four people were in line. While waiting, he checked his messages. He didn't look up from his phone until he heard a voice say, "Hello sir, you're next. How may I assist you today?"

The soft and melodious voice grabbed his attention, but when he glanced up and saw the face that spoke those words he was stunned by her beauty. It wasn't a beauty derived from thousands of dollars of cosmetic injections or from the hands of a skillful aesthetician who meticulously shaped and highlighted every part of her face like the treatments his sister regularly received.

Instead this woman's natural beauty came from a splash of freckles across her nose and cheeks, sparkling

13

green eyes, and auburn hair that glistened with golden highlights making it look as if it were drenched in a sunset.

Her self-confidence was evident through her crisp Rothwell's uniform and precisely aligned posture. He imagined her bantering with friends on a vast number of topics rather than the banal conversations he was accustomed to hearing from the socialites in his elite circle, which centered on the newest outfit or the latest gossip.

This was a woman he wanted to get to know more about. Finally realizing he was standing there looking like a statue, he gave her a slight grin. He strode forward and placed the shopping bag on the counter. "Hello, I wish to return this scarf. The receipt is in the bag."

Natalie smiled. "It's my pleasure to serve you. Did the design not suit your girlfriend or wife? Would you like some assistance in finding something more suitable?"

Alexander pretended to have a cough to stop himself from laughing. His first reaction was to say it was his sister's choice, but then remembered he was playing a role. "No, I'm one of Rothwell's personal shoppers. By having me take care of these mundane chores, my client can leverage her time more effectively. That's just one of the benefits of having a shopper."

Natalie's eyes brightened. "Are you a new hire like me?"

"Um, yes. I've been a shopper here for, um, about a week. Is this your regular department?"

"No, I'm a fill-in for today. The department manager who was scheduled to train me is sick. Not sure where I'll be tomorrow."

"But you will be here tomorrow. What department will you be working in? I'm sure whatever it is, you'll be great." Alexander stopped and took a breath to keep himself from babbling. What is wrong with me? Why do I feel so tongue tied? I don't want her think I'm an idiot and avoid me the next time I see her. That can't happen. "How about celebrating your first day on the job by having tea or coffee with me at "Bites," the store's tea room? Or have lunch with me? Statistically speaking, a work break is effective for improving both well-being and performance. So it would be good for both you and the company."

Natalie giggled. "Sounds like it would be very beneficial all around." She glanced at her watch. "My lunch break is scheduled in 2 hours 15 minutes."

"That will work for me. I'll reserve a table and meet you there. What's your name?"

"Natalie Baynton. Yours?"

"Alex…White." As he took the credit receipt from her, their fingers met, and a jolt of electricity passed between them, and he broke out in a big grin. "That was electrifying. Wonder what sparks our lunch chat will have? See you soon."

As he calmly walked away, his eyes danced with delight. I like the way this day has started.

# Chapter 3

## Natalie

Natalie wondered what her first day of work would be like as she meticulously dressed and applied just a slight hint of makeup to enhance her features. Although her sleep had been erratic like a child anticipating Christmas morning, her adrenaline was pumping.

She reread the introduction notes in her binder for the first day and made sure her store-supplied basic purse with her name tag contained multiple pens, breath mints, comb, mirror, lipstick, fresh scented hand sanitizer and her wallet. Breakfast and dinner were available at their employee housing and was provided free of charge, but lunch would be her own expense.

When she and Lauren arrived at the cafeteria, the room was full of boisterous chatter. The aroma of sizzling bacon and sausage mixed with the scent of freshly baked bread and brewed coffee awakened their taste buds. The line for food moved quickly and despite the fact it was already crowded, they found an empty table.

When Natalie sat and placed her food tray on the table she whispered to Lauren, "Would it be okay if I said a prayer before we eat?" Lauren nodded in agreement. In a soft voice heard only between the two of them Natalie began, "Heavenly Father, we thank you for this job opportunity you have given us. Guide our hearts and minds to do the best in our work. We thank you for this food and the blessing of this day. In Jesus's name. Amen."

Laura reached over and squeezed Natalie's hand. "Thanks for suggesting prayer. I'm a bit nervous and I needed that reminder to thank God for this opportunity."

Natalie cast glances between her full plate of food and Laura's, which consisted of an egg white omelet with spinach and herbal tea with lemon. "That's really all you're eating?"

Laura shrugged. "My normal protein shake wasn't an option, so I'm splurging with an omelet. Should probably add 500 more steps because of that.'

"If that's a splurge, then I must look like a piggy to you."

"No not at all. That's how normal people eat. When I can make more money outside of modeling, I'll be able to eat like that, too."

In a whisper, Natalie asked, "You don't have any issues with bulimia, do you?"

"No, I know how bad that is for my health. If you ever catch me falling into that eating disorder, stop me."

"Agreed. And if you catch me binge eating because I'm getting too stressed with work, make sure I de-stress by exercise instead."

"Deal. Have you noticed the guys in here? More women than men, but a number of men are definitely hotties. But I think the best dating prospects will be our customers. If they can afford to shop at Rothwell's, they have money. That makes for great dating potential."

"If I decide to date again, he wouldn't have to be rich. I want someone who's fun to be with, easy to talk to, and goal oriented. Someone I can trust and count on." As Natalie picked up her fork her eyes narrowed as her thoughts drifted back to Jake the Snake, as she preferred to think of him these days. At the beginning he was fun, and they texted each other multiple times daily. He was impressed that she was working and going to college but thought a business or law degree, like he had, would have been more worthwhile than a fashion one.

When her work shifts left her exhausted and too tired to go to company functions with him, he got grumpy. The only thing he appreciated about her job was the fact she could buy him clothes with her store discount. The last set of clothes he reimbursed her for was for an alleged 4-day getaway for team building. But she discovered the team was only Jake and one of the female partners in the firm he'd latched onto in hopes of getting a promotion and more money. That was the end of their relationship. And she wasn't ready to start another one.

After breakfast, Natalie and Laura headed to their orientation for Rothwell's employees. From there, they were directed to the areas for picking up their uniforms according to the measurements they had given on their paperwork. When Laura picked up her two sets of suits, she whispered, "Wow, these uniforms are really classy. The wool is so soft. Feels almost like cashmere. The blouses drape like silk. I'm gonna like getting dressed for work. And these short pumps will be easy to wear all day."

Excited, they followed the crowd of employees to their dressing area to change into their new attire. Their regular clothes were stored in their personal lockers before heading to their daily assignments.

Natalie was disappointed that her first assignment was in the returns department, rather than something more aligned with her degree and work history. However, one of the trainers was sick and they were short-staffed in this department. Still she'd do her best to show she was committed to the job no matter what area she was assigned.

Prior to the store opening, the department manager gave her a short orientation on the store's rules for tallying the receipts correctly in the register, sorting the returns, and providing credits in a professional and friendly manner. For the first 30 minutes, she observed how her trainer handled irritable customers, then she was left on her own. Since it was early in the day foot traffic in her department was low until a flurry of customers fell into line. And that's when she met Alex.

She initially pegged him as one of the upscale store patrons as he stood in line texting. He wore a deep brown leather lambskin jacket with an Aran Knit sweater underneath, tan corduroy pants, and Chelsea boots. His attire probably cost more than her week's pay. When she directed him to her counter he just stood there staring at her – not in a leering way, but as if he were trying to figure out who she was. Their gazes locked. She was mesmerized by those eyes. They were the color of stormy seas that held a magnetic allure. And his sun-kissed, tousled tawny brown hair were something she wanted to run her fingers through. She tried to push her immediate attraction to him away, but when he spoke in that distinct clipped British accent, she always adored in romance movies, she was hooked.

She secretly hoped he'd be an absolute jerk to break the spell, but he was cute and charming. Their conversation lasted only a few minutes yet during that time he managed to ask her to share lunch with him. Had he been a customer she would have felt it necessary to turn him down. But Alex said he was a personal shopper for the store and still bumbling through what needed to be done. Since they were both newbies, he thought it would be fun to be able to chat over lunch about their workday. And to her surprise she agreed. She just couldn't resist that British accent.

When the next customer came up to her counter, Natalie put on her best professional demeanor though her cheeks felt a bit flushed. Competently working through the returns for the next two customers, she couldn't stop thinking about Alex. What in the world am I doing flirting with another employee? Sure he looked like one of those celebrities I'd expect to see on the cover of GQ magazine. And that aristocratic British accent was swoonable. It felt like being in a rom-com with the likes of Hugh Grant, or Henry Golding. How could I pass up seeing him again? It's only lunch. Maybe we'll just chat and then only see each other again in passing as we work. This job needs to be my #1 focus and not getting involved in some starry-eyed romance I don't have time for or need.

# Chapter 4

## Lunch Together

Alex arrived at Rothwell's tea room, "Bites, Bubbles, and Treats" fifteen minutes early to ensure the specific seating assignment he requested was provided. As he walked to the table, he scanned the room confirming no one in upper management who knew him were there. His table was in the back of the restaurant and had a partially obscured view of the person sitting there. However, leaning back slightly, anyone entering the restaurant was visible.

As he perused the menu, his right thumb rubbed against the back of the ring on his fourth finger. The gold ring with a square natural emerald had been passed down from his great-grandfather and he always wore it. It had a sturdy feel to it, like the man who had originally owned it. As a stock broker, he survived and thrived after the crash of 1929. He taught his money strategies to his son and grandson.

Now he was breaking that family tradition by choosing to work at his uncle's store. His father kept hoping he'd change his career choice. Alexander hoped once his parents came to visit in December, they'd see this was the right career for him.

When he saw Natalie arrive, he strode toward her not wanting to miss a minute of their time together. Her eyes sparkled as she walked toward him.

"I'm early, but I guess you're between your personal shopping assignments," Natalie said as Alex put his hand on the small of her back and motioned to their table. She stiffened up for a moment remembering the way her ex-boyfriend used that slight pressure of his hand on her back to keep her on course when they were going somewhere. She quickly relaxed realizing Alex's touch was softer and not as insistent.

A waiter arrived at their table within a minute of being seated. Their drink order consisted of a bottle of Rothwell's sparkling water for Alex and Earl Grey tea for Natalie.

"Sparkling water and not tea?" Natalie asked as she tilted her head.

With a hint of merriment in his eyes, he tapped his hand over his heart. "Are you stereotyping me as a tea drinker since I'm a Brit?"

Natalie's hand jumped to her lips. "I'm so sorry. That was a quick assumption."

"Not a problem. Did you know that a recent consumer survey showed  63% of Brits drink coffee regularly, while only 59% regularly drink tea. I do drink tea often, but I enjoy the fizz of sparking water. The bubbles makes me feel like I'm celebrating something, which I am in welcoming you to the store."

"My, that sounded a bit imperious as if you were in charge of it."

Alex covered his hand in a cough to start from sputtering. "Me? In charge? Don't I wish. I've only been here a few days. No grand promotions yet."

"Yes, of course," Natalie smirked. "So what would you suggest I order with your vast knowledge of the store?"

"They have a wonderful butternut squash soup with bits of apple, a hint of sage and drizzled with sherry cream. And the beet salad with field greens, pecans, and goat cheese is also lovely. Do you have any dietary preferences?"

"No, not me. If it looks good on the plate, I'm willing to give it a try. How about you?"

"Yes, I like trying new dishes. The offerings of wild game found here in Aspen are quite delicious. So, I think the smoked venison stew on the menu will be my choice."

"Your suggestion of the soup and salad sounds good. I'll go with them."

Once their drinks arrived and meal orders taken, Alex's attention returned to Natalie. Their conversation flowed freely. They delved into each other's favorite foods - his was steak and kidney pie and hers was chicken piccata. Both said they enjoyed apple pie as a dessert but did not agree if it should come with ice cream or a thick slice of cheese. For dislikes, he said mint jelly should never be served with a meat and she said mayonnaise should never be on a sandwich.

His favorite sports to follow were rugby and cricket, while hers were skiing contests and watching the Super bowl for the halftime show and funny commercials.

But those questions were softball topics. The unasked ones Natalie wanted to know the answers to were about past or present girlfriends. However, she did learn he was a permanent employee, which made her smile. If a relationship developed it could move at a slow pace. Of course she wasn't interested in a romance, but it was good to know potential options.

Too soon Natalie's phone beeped letting her know her break was almost over.. Alex paid cash for the meal. Her past boyfriends always paid by credit card. If she had paid the bill, there would be only a few dollars left in her purse. But he showed no concern about being short on funds as he slipped his copy of the receipt in his wallet.

As they rose from the table, Alex let her take the lead so he could continue to be on the lookout for the few executive board members who knew his real name. Had they appeared, he had an excuse ready to whisper to Natalie to make a quick exit.

Alex wished he could draw her in for a kiss to see what those lush lips would feel like, but that would wait for another time. And there would be another time. As he leaned closer to chat, he caught her perfume's floral hints. He breathed the scent in for a moment to remember, then straightened his posture. "I've got reports that'll keep me busy tonight and tomorrow. May I suggest we meet again then to share our work stories?"

Her almost instant smile and nod warmed him from his head to his toes.

"Let's exchange numbers so we don't have to search the store to find each other."

Natalie lowered her head for a moment and bit her lip, which made Alex fear that he'd misread her reactions. Then she raised her head and gave a hint of a smile. "I'd like that."

Alex beamed. "Great. Let's meet here again and we'll figure out the time."

After they exchanged numbers, Natalie glanced at her watch. "Oops. Need to go. See you soon. Then she gave a short wave and turned to walk away.

Alex called out. "Wait. What is the scent you are wearing? It suits you."

"Thanks. It's Dolce & Gabbana Light Blue."

Alex jotted a note into his phone. "Find floral scents in D&G lite blue. Get bouquet for her hotel room." Then he shook his head. *I don't even know where she lives. But that doesn't matter. We'll be seeing each other again soon. That's something to definitely look forward to..*

# Chapter 5

## Dinner with Emma and Alex

Two weeks later, Alex and Emma dined at one of the trendy restaurants in town, which was Emma's choice. While they ate, she scanned the room for celebrities. Spotting a famous face, she whispered to her brother. "The table three over from us? Isn't that Thani Fitzhiggins? Love that blouse she's wearing. It's a Chloe, if I'm not mistaken. And that gorgeous guy seated across from her is Toby Everson. They were co-stars in that latest thriller that had box office success. It's rumored that they had an affair on the set. They certainly look cozy. I wonder what other celebrities we might see tonight."

"Really Emma? Did you want to come here for the food? Or was it just to do celebrity sighting?"

"Dear brother, don't go all lofty on me. You've looked when I pointed out the celebrities. It keeps me from being bored." She paused for a moment and pouted but still had a twinkle in her eyes. "You're always busy. Is Uncle Will working you like a slave driver? You don't even have time to lunch with me."

"Uncle Will keeps me busy, but I'm enjoying it. It actually energizes me. You know how I love statistics and analysis." He raised an eyebrow and tapped his finger on the table. "How I'm enjoying my lunch time is a different story."

"My, that sounds a bit mysterious. Do tell."

"Remember when you asked me to return that scarf?"

"Yes, and I quickly reused the gift card you received and bought more."

"Of course you did. You do love to shop. But back to the return I made. The woman who assisted me was fascinating. We had lunch together that day and most days since then. She's very keen on the store and is training to become a fashion buyer."

"Does she know who you are?"

"I told her my name was Alex White and I worked as a personal shopper."

"Alexander, tell me you're not going to use the store's employees as your shopping cart for finding your next fling?"

"No, I'm not like that anymore. I'm serious about my work. I don't have time for partying and having a new girlfriend every season."

"What's this person like who has captured your attention?

"She's totally different from my regular socialites. She's career focused. I like her... a lot. She is a breath of fresh air."

"Then don't break her heart and destroy her dreams."

"I'm not into being the playboy anymore. These past few years working with Uncle Will have made me more serious about my career. Now he's given me the opportunity to become the CFO at this location once the current man retires in January."

"When are you planning on telling Daddy that working with Uncle Will is permanent and not a passing fancy? You know he's still hoping you'll sign on at his firm selling stocks and securities?"

"I want to do it in person when he and Mummy arrive for the Christmas Charity Ball. I can show him what I have planned. I want him to see this is where I'm belong, not as his clone."

"And what about this girl? Will you tell Mummy that you're seeing a working class American?"

"Emma, she has both an undergrad and master's degree. She's working her way up in management."

Emma waved her hand in the air dismissively. "Fine, she's middle-class. Mummy will still think she's below us."

"When she arrives, I will make sure she sees how wonderful Natalie is."

"She's really gotten under your skin. When do I get to meet her?"

Alex raised an eyebrow. "Don't give me that mischievous look. I don't want you interfering with Natalie and me. You'll meet her in my time. I'll give her fair warning about how to deal with you before that."

"Fine. Keep her a secret for now. I'll keep myself busy looking for someone dashing to be my escort at the Christmas Ball."

Alex imagined how lovely Natalie would look in a formal gown at that ball, then shook his head. No time for daydreams. Got to focus on my new job. Finding the right words to tell my parents about why I chose this position over the family business. Lord grant me your wisdom. I'm going to need it.

# Chapter 6

## Executive Board Meeting

Alex spent the next day reviewing Rothwell's charts and reports in his hotel room. There would be a board meeting in the executive offices later in the afternoon. When he finally took a break and ordered room service, he thought about the discussion yesterday with his sister. Her words came back to him as if she were there with him.

"Alexander, I'll always be your best cheerleader, but I don't want you to make a mess of things. You've had many past flirtations with an assortment of theater actresses and socialites. You can't do that with the female employees at the store or hotel. That could cause problems for Uncle Will."

He cringed thinking of the times he considered women as nothing more than disposable playthings in his early 20s. That all changed when a friend challenged him to re-evaluate his life, accept he was a sinner, and ask for God's forgiveness. Now he was following God's will for his life. Though his sister wasn't keen on him dating someone outside of his social class, and an American to boot, he felt differently. Natalie was so inquisitive, and he loved the way her eyes lit up when she learned something new.

Knowing she had little time to chat at work, He sent her a short text to keep in touch.

> **Alex:** Busy Day. Time for next appointment. See you tomorrow at lunch.

A few minutes later, he got a response.

> **Natalie:** Busy, but good day for me. Let's compare work notes tomorrow. No scratch that. Let's talk about fun stuff to do in Aspen.

He grinned imagining her saying that in her soft and cheery voice. Though he wanted to linger on that thought, it was time to get back to work. Opening his computer to the list of upper management department heads, he reviewed their pictures, names, and details committing them to memory so he wouldn't get lost in the myriads of introductions his uncle would be making at today's special board meeting. They knew Stefan Dubicki was retiring as the CFO, but as yet no name had been mentioned as his replacement.

For now, he would be introduced as a consultant. This meeting was a brainstorming session to bounce around ideas to improve the company's bottom line. After that, he'd be meeting them individually to see how their management styles could mesh together. Since he had already familiarized himself with the details of operating the company, he hoped that it would dispel any issues of nepotism.

Adding a jacket and tie to the tailored white shirt and dress pants already worn, he reviewed his appearance in the mirror. Responding to the text message saying his car was ready downstairs, he left. While in the elevator, he silently prayed, *God guide me as I face this new challenge.*

Upon entering the store, he wished he could stop and see Natalie, but his attire might bring up questions we wasn't ready to answer. Instead, he strode to the private elevator for his uncle's office and boardroom and inserted the special key card.

This event was the upper level management "happy hour" of sorts. A plethora of appetizers and drinks were available, and music played softly in the background. It had an informal atmosphere so that everyone could relax but not to the point of getting drunk and being obnoxious. Alex heard a mix of voices and music even before he entered the room. His uncle had apparently been on the lookout for his entrance, and he immediately waved him over to where he stood chatting with two other men.

"Alexander, I'd like to introduce you to Stefan Dubicki, my CFO and Neal Philmar, our Facilities Manager."

"Pleased to meet you both. I've heard good things from Sir William on how capable the two of you are in your jobs."

Sir William put his hand on Alexander's shoulder. "Alexander started as an intern with my company and continued throughout both his undergraduate schooling and master's degree programs. For the last two years, he's handled operations at one of my other businesses and increased my profits substantially. He's here as a consultant and is interested in learning the ideas everyone has to improve our Aspen operations."

The two men were allowed to pepper Alexander with several questions until his uncle decided it was time for him to meet other managers. Introductions and questioning kept his wits alert for the next 90 minutes. He felt he made a good impression and prayed that his inclusion at the top of this management group would be a smooth one.

# Chapter 7

## The Elevator Mistake

The next day at lunchtime, Alex entered the store and immediately sent Natalie a text.

**Alex:** You on a break?

While waiting for a response, he glanced around the area to see if she'd be walking by. A few minutes later, he heard the pinged response of a text.

**Natalie:** No. In the warehouse. Sorting through shipment of evening gowns.

**Alex:** Tell me about them over lunch?

**Natalie:** 1 pm still work?

**Alex:** Yes. See you at Bites.

**Natalie:** Soon!

His heart beat a little faster thinking about seeing Natalie. How could two days apart seem so long? He was early for his appointment with his uncle. Rather than sit in the lobby, he walked through a few departments taking note of the foot traffic and the number of store's shopping bags seen. The shopping bags didn't tell the whole story. Since Rothwell's provided delivery of packages for their hotel guests, they wouldn't be hindered from doing additional shopping. The store provided other events to uptick revenues as well. The gowns Natalie was sorting through were likely those for the gala Christmas fashion show.

When his phone intoned the music showing it was his uncle, he hastened his pace to find a quiet spot nearby and answered the call.

"Are you in the store, Alexander?"

"Yes. Shopping as you've suggested."

"Come up now. My receptionist is at lunch. So head directly to my office."

"On my way."

When he stepped out of the private elevator and strode down the hall to his uncle's office, he glanced toward the boardroom that held the management reception the night before. Everything had been put back in place and was ship-shape and Bristol fashion. The same could be said of his uncle's office. This space showed his personal taste. The floors were a lustrous red oak. His desk and bookcases were crafted in solid maple with swirled burl panels. The credenza behind the desk held pictures of his uncle and various celebrities at charity fundraisers. The walls held oil paintings of sailing races and skiing – which were his two favorite sports.

His uncle rose from his tufted leather chair to shake his hand and greet him, then motioned for him to sit in one of the two plush swivel leather chairs in front of the desk. "What were your impressions of meeting my team last night?"

"They are indeed a formidable group, and no doubt are already wondering why I'm here rather than in one of your other locations."

Sir William smirked. "No doubt the rumor mills are working overtime today. Do you think you'll have any problems working with Stefan during the transition?"

"No not at all. He reminds me of one of my favorite professors at Cambridge who hammered into me the importance of meticulously studying the details in reports. I think we'll get along quite well. But what will they think of having a 30 something replacing a 30 year veteran with the company?"

"You're taking this position because you are capable of handling it. Any ruffled feathers will be my problem, not yours. Now tell me how you and Emma are enjoying yourselves while you're here?"

Alexander leaned back in his chair and rolled his eyes. "Emma is thoroughly enjoying the shopping. And she's enamored with the celebrity sightings. I enjoy the high energy and excitement around the store and the hotel. I think the key to this location is making sure you don't have staff turnovers in the off season."

"I'm glad you brought that up. Let me show you some of the ideas I have to help make the off months more profitable. You know the X Games are here in the winter. I've been making contacts to include other events during spring and summer."

For the next 40 minutes, the two men went back and forth trading ideas for how they could improve the resort and store traffic in the off season. It wasn't until Alexander glanced at his watch that he noticed how much time had elapsed. His lunch with Natalie was in 5 minutes. He nodded to his uncle's last response, then he stood and reached over to shake his uncle's hand. "Thanks for chatting with me. I know you're busy, so I won't take any more of your time."

Sir William gave him an appraising look. "Are you late for an appointment? I haven't scheduled any meetings for you, so what is it?"

"I have a lunch date with a lovely lady. I don't want to keep her waiting."

"Then get going. Let the ideas we shared percolate in your brain for a couple of days. Let me know if you come up with others."

"Thanks, sir." Alexander turned and rushed out of the office to the elevator. He should just be able to get there in time.

***

As soon as the elevator doors opened on the main floor, Alex rushed out. Hearing Natalie call his name, he caught his breath. She saw him get off the elevator -- an elevator he would have no reason to use. Think! He turned with a big smile on his face. "How's this for timing? We run into each other before we even get to the restaurant. More time to chat as we walk.

"What are you doing getting off that elevator. That's for the executive offices. You need a special key card to access it."

"Really? W-w-why would you think I'd, uhh, have a key card. You know, ummm, I'm just a personal shopper."

"Right, but customers don't have key card access. What gives?"

"Nothing. Had to drop a thank you gift to the head office from guest services. Let's get some lunch. I'm famished."

"That still doesn't explain the key card access. You can't just press a button and go up."

Alex shrugged. "When I got there someone was exiting. I caught the door before it closed. No big thing."

"Still sounds strange to me."

"It's really nothing. Here we are at the restaurant already." Alex gave his name to the host at the podium. As they walked to the table, he silently wished their lunch conversation would make Natalie forget about seeing him at that elevator.

# Chapter 8

## Natalie and Laura Discussion

Still pondering seeing Alex step out of the executive elevator, Natalie sipped her hot cocoa and turned to Laura as they sat on their couch. "Have you ever delivered anything to the executive office for a manager?"

"No, why would I do that?" Laura took a sip of her no-calorie hot water and lemon. "We can't get there on the regular elevators."

"Right. But I saw Alex get out of the private elevator as we headed to lunch."

"Did a manager get off the elevator with him? Oh, wait. You had lunch with him again?"

Natalie smiled and nodded. "Yes, it's a daily event."

"That sounds promising."

Her heart fluttered. "It is. But back to the elevator. He told me he was delivering something. Made it seem like no big deal. Still seems odd to me."

"Don't overthink this. Accept it as no big deal as Alex says."

Natalie let out a deep breath and settled back into the couch cushions. "I guess so."

Laura leaned forward. "When do I get to meet this guy?"

"It's hard to say with our work schedules." Then she wagged a finger at her roommate. "And you don't get to be a third person on our lunch dates. Our time goes by too quickly. However, we talked about Thanksgiving, which is less than a week away. The store is closed. We'll have the whole day free. The cafeteria downstairs will probably have some sort of Thanksgiving spread."

Then she paused and grinned like a Cheshire cat. "Or we could go to Rothwell's Hotel and enjoy their Thanksgiving buffet. Alex can snag three complimentary dinner passes from their concierge.. He's apparently pretty tight with him as they both cater to guests' special requests."

Laura's mouth fell open, and her eyes grew wide. "That's incredible. I've heard they do lavish buffets. I'll only be able to nibble a bit of this and that. Need to still fit into the evening gowns for the fashion show without showing a tummy bulge. No matter. I'll enjoy it vicariously by watching what you choose to eat while I scope out worthwhile dating material."

"We'll have to dress up since it's a special event."

Laura jumped up and made a beeline for the bedroom. "It's got to be something festive. With velvet or sequins. Silver or gold threads. And definitely heels."

Natalie quickly followed behind. "I have a dark green cashmere sweater with a beaded scoop neckline which I could pair with a black velvet side slit midi or black suede pants."

Each of them pulled out a number of separates from their closets and drawers and tossed them on the bed as they began to compare and contrast which items would work best together.

Laura held up to two items for approval.

Natalie pointed to the one on her right and nodded. "Which do you like better? Sweater or silky knit."

"Silk knit. Since you're already paired up, maybe Alex could point out some potential options for me. Is he working with any single hottie guys with lots of money? Being a hottie isn't required. He could be a nerdy type with money."

"He doesn't mention his clients. We don't talk about business much. But maybe he knows someone who could make a good fourth person for our table."

Laura pushed aside some of the clothes on the bed and sat. "I'm envious of how quickly the two of you fell together. So far, no one has caught my attention. So many of the guys that come into the store already have someone on their arm. The pickings are slim. Or maybe I'm being too picky. It sure would be nice to find somebody special to cuddle up with for Christmas and New Year's."

At the mention of Christmas and New Year's, Natalie imagined herself relaxing on a soft leather couch with Alex, facing a roaring fireplace, drinking hot cocoa and exchanging gifts. Natalie shook her head and silently laughed. What is happening to me? I'm creating a scene with the two of us like we're in some romance movie. The only reality in that vision would be sitting on these couches, sipping hot cocoa, and watching a fireplace scene on TV. I love being with Alex, but I don't know if what we started will last. My job needs to be my focus, not melting down like a snowman by falling in love.

# Chapter 9

## Thanksgiving Dinner

On Thanksgiving Day, Alex arranged for one of Rothwell's hotel limos to pick up Laura and Natalie. The driver parked to the side of the entrance as he went upstairs to get them. When Natalie opened the door to their mini-suite, he stared at her in amazement. "Wow. You look stunning. I don't know how any of the other guys will be able to keep their eyes off you."

From inside the room, another voice replied, "I certainly hope they can. Other women will be there, including me."

Alex leaned close and gave Natalie a soft kiss on her cheek. "I take it that's your roommate."

Natalie took his hand and pulled him inside. With a twinkle in her eyes she added, "Yes, this is Laura. She's wanted to meet you to see if she approves of us going out."

Alex pulled Natalie close to his side and did a slight bow. "Do I meet your approval?"

Laura crossed one arm over her chest, tapped her other hand to her chin and narrowed her eyes. "Hmmm. You're nicely dressed, have a great smile, and your Brit accent is quite charming. But seeing the way the two of you look at each other shows you're a match. Now let's see if I can find my perfect match. Got any suggestions?"

Alex sputtered, "I'm hardly qualified to be a matchmaker. You'd be better matched by one of the many dating apps. Would you like me to do an analysis of which ones are best?"

Natalie laughed and playfully tapped his arm. "Pay no attention to her. She asks me that every day. Guys are always hitting on her. She's quite picky."

"Dining at fabulous restaurants with a date doesn't thrill me. Can't eat much. I need to keep my model figure." Laura performed a perfect model turn and pivot to make her point.

Can't go skiing for fear of broken bones, but I love theater, shows, and sparkling gifts."

"See what I mean? She's hoping to find a Prince Charming. One day perhaps she will." Natalie winked at Laura. "Just hope she notices him when he shows up."

Alex grinned. "Wish I could be of assistance, but no one comes to mind. If they do, I'll tell Natalie. Now let's go so we're not late for our reservation."

"But RFTA doesn't come for at least another 15 minutes. Wouldn't it be better just to wait here?" Natalie asked.

Alex winked at Natalie. "Get your coats. I've got a car to take us to the hotel since this a special occasion."

Laura gave him a thumbs up. "I like this guy."

As they exited the double glass doors to the street, Natalie asked, "What kind of car were you able to rent for the day?"

"You'll see." He punched some numbers into his phone. "Come around to the front now." As the limo pulled to the front curb, The driver got out and opened the passenger doors.

Laura's eyes grew large, and she gasped. "How did you get a limo from Rothwell's?"

"This is hardly one of the perks of being a personal shopper." Natalie whispered in his ear.

As they drove away, Alex said, "It's who you know. There is regular shuttle service between the hotel and the store for guests. Since the store is closed, I knew it would be easy to find one available. Cade Jackson, the hotel concierge, arranged the service for me."

"But you're not a hotel guest." Natalie said.

Alex's pulse quickened. He was a hotel guest but didn't want Natalie to know at this point. It would be another expense he couldn't explain in regard to his alleged personal shopper job. In reality, he was able to get the limo by paying a generous tip to Cade and the driver. "Of course not, but I do a lot of going back and forth to the hotel and store as part of being a personal shopper. Cade's work and mine overlap at times so we've gotten to be friends."

"He sounds like a good friend to have. I'd like to meet him," Laura said.

"He's working today managing any last minute details for Americans with special Thanksgiving requests. Once we're seated, I'll let you ladies get your beverages and peruse the food choices while I see if he's at his desk."

As they entered the hotel, there was a constant flow of guests and staff gliding across the brown and gold marble floors of the foyer. Soft jazz music played in the background. Fresh pine garlands draped the tall windows and poinsettias circled around the 12-foot Christmas tree adorned with sparkling white lights. A magnificent Chihuly blown glass chandelier hung from the high ceiling with tendrils of orange and yellow that looked like a blazing sun. Natalie whispered to Alex, "This hotel is gorgeous. Can't wait to see the restaurant."

When they arrived at the restaurant, they had to wait a few minutes for the maître d' to assign a host to take them to their table. Peering into the restaurant they could see the white clothed tables surrounded by leather club chairs. Red oak wainscoting covered the lower walls while the upper sections were a textured pale beige that had the appearance of suede.

Once they were seated and Alex left, Laura whispered to Natalie. "Alex sure has the right connections. If you ever get tired of him, I'll take your place. Too bad he doesn't have a brother."

Natalie flashed a smile. "Sometimes it's hard for me to concentrate on work without thoughts of his smile or laughter popping in my head." *But I can't let a romance have me lose my focus on becoming a fashion buyer.*

"Look at the people around us. They're wearing Dior, Marc Jacobs, Gucci, and Prada. They can afford this. Alex's clothes look like designer brands, but I'm not that familiar with Brit designers. He's very charming with his proper Brit accent, but I wonder if there's more to him than you know."

"Weren't you the one who told me not to overthink the elevator thing. Aren't you doing the same thing?"

"Hey…I'm just saying Alex might have a secret or two he's hiding."

"The job I want with Rothwell's might require a transfer to another store. For now, I have to consider our relationship as temporary. If it's God's will for it to be long-lasting, he'll need to show a way to make it work." She pushed back her chair and stood. "Now let's take a look at the food choices before my tummy starts growling."

Laura leaned close and whispered as they walked. "Look straight ahead and to the right at the table at the edge of the floor to ceiling window. I believe that's one of the judges for that talent show called 'America's Next Big Name.' Love the luster on her blue print silk top. And the guy is...can't remember his name. No wait that's the guy who plays the lead in that new counter-terrorist-secret-agent movie. I wouldn't mind him protecting me."

Natalie rolled her eyes and whispered back. "Knowing you, you'll probably sight a couple more celebrities in the dining room today."

# Chapter 10

## *Alexander*

While Natalie and Laura were in the restaurant, Alex waited patiently for the client with Cade to finish. He had told the truth about being friends with Cade, but it began with the discovery of both graduating from the same university in England. Cade's full name was Charles Cavender Jackson, but his nickname became Cade and he kept it.

When Cade nodded his head, Alex came over to his desk and sat. "Busy day?"

Cade shrugged. "Not really. What can I do for you?"

"Thanks for finding a spot for us in the dining room. I know this day can easily overbook. My girlfriend and her roommate think the dinner buffet is a complimentary perk I got. I don't want them to know I paid for it."

"Why's that?"

"Because I'd have to explain how I could afford to pay for the meals as well as having a suite at the hotel. When I met Natalie, she mistook me for another store employee. Probably because I told her so."

"You don't work at the store? You are always a requesting a car to take you there. Are you stalking her?"

"Heavens no. I will be working there. Only I'm unofficial for now. The announcement will come at Sir Willliams Charity Ball. Are you coming?"

Cade rolled his eyes. "Sorry, $2,000 is a bit pricey for a date for me."

Alex waved his hand dismissively. "You've been a great help in getting a number of prizes for the silent auction. What they'll bring in will more than compensate for those ticket prices. I'll confirm it with Sir William. Have you a lady in mind to escort?"

"I noticed you brought in two ladies. I can see the redhead is your date. What's the status of the other woman?"

"Status? She's American. A model for the store."

"I had a feeling she was a model by her graceful walk. Think she'd like to go with me?"

"I know she would love going to the ball. Like my sister, she's enamored with seeking out celebrities. You'd be high on her list if you could point them out and tell her stories of your dealings with high-profile guests here but keep their names anonymous."

Cade nodded his head and smiled. "Oh I could definitely tell some stories."

"Great. When you get a break, join us at our table."

"Sure."

"When you drop by, I'll introduce you and let you charm her for a few minutes. But don't mention the ball yet. Wait for that as a second or third date." Alex glanced at his watch. "Best be getting back to them."

"See you soon."

Alex began walking away, then turned, "Oh, one last thing. The roommate loves a Brit accent. Not a surprise as some polls list a British accent in the top 3 foreign accents people find most attractive."

Cade came to their table about 30 minutes later. He leaned against the empty chair at the table and faced the two females. "I trust you are enjoying your meal and being part of the who's who of our restaurant."

Hearing Cade's accent, Laura gazed at him with rapt attention. She had expected him to be one of those avid skiers born and raised In Colorado. His face had a reddish glow probably from skiing, broad shoulders, an aquiline nose, short wavy brown hair, and hazel eyes that were an enthralling blend of earthy browns and hints of green.

"Yes, it's wonderful and so elegant. Have you had a chance to try any of the food?" Laura asked, keeping her eyes only on him.

"No, that will have to wait till a bit later. I'm still on duty. Just wanted to stop by and say hello."

"I'm glad you did. Too bad you can't join us." Laura patted the chair beside her. "As you can see we have an empty seat."

For a few seconds more than needed, Cade and Laura locked eyes with each other.

Alex cleared his throat. "Please excuse my poor manners for not making introductions. Cade, this is my girlfriend Natalie and her roommate, Laura. They both work at the store. Natalie is working in women's fashion watching the buying trends and formulating ideas for what Rothwell's should purchase next. Laura is one of the models who helps make those clothing lines look great, so they'll sell more of them."

Cade smiled at Laura. "Yes, I can see that you would. I'll have to pop over to the store and see one of those impromptu modeling shows that so many of the guests are talking about."

"They're not really that impromptu. We usually schedule them when foot traffic dips a bit to create energy and enthusiasm. I don't know what's scheduled for tomorrow. It is the big start of the Christmas buying frenzy…" She picked up her phone. "but I could send you a text."

"Cade held out his hand. "May I add my number to your phone now?"

"Of course." As their fingertips touched in the transfer, Laura felt a tingle go up her arm and heat rise on her face.

"Done." Cade glanced at his phone which started buzzing. "Sorry, need to take care of business. Enjoy the rest of your meal." Then he gave a short bow to Laura and Natalie and left.

Laura sighed as she watched him leave. "I did not expect a British accent. Thought he was a local." Then her head swiveled to face Alex. "Do you know where he's from?"

"Funny you should ask. In one of our chats, we discovered that we both graduated from Bath University. He was a year behind me. If I recall properly, I believe he said he grew up in Swindon. That's between Bath and London."

"What's his degree in?"

"Believe it or not, it's computer science. He's a genius when it comes to computers, but he loves the challenge of his work here." Alex sighed and shook his head. "He could do so much more in the executive department. He'd be more of an asset there than here."

Natalie jabbed an elbow at Laura. "You sure seem to have taken a big interest in somebody you just met. Does he merit potential for a date?"

Laura's eyes twinkled. "Under that jacket I sense there's muscles. And the accent got to me. If he's a whiz with computers, he's no dummy." She frowned and turned to Alex. "I wasn't too pushy getting his phone number, was I?"

Alex leaned back and chuckled softly. I think he was trying to come up with a way to ask for your phone number. You beat him to it."

"Oh my, yes, Laura," Natalie added. "The way the two of you looked at each other it was as if nobody else was in the room."

Laura mused. "Hmmm. I like that. Hope he'll come to one of the modeling shows. I'd like to spend more time with him."

# Chapter 11

## Planning for Christmas

With the official start of the holiday season, Natalie's work day became long and hectic. She now had charge of scheduling and overseeing the pop up events plus finalizing the details for the Gala Christmas fashion show.

Alex was spending a lot of time in the executive office strategizing with both Sir William and Stefan. Though he hadn't been named Stefan's replacement, it was pretty obvious by the amount of time the three men spent together that something was happening.

Even with both their busy schedules, Natalie and Alex still found time to share lunch together. Sometimes it was in "Bites" and others at the snack bar. They were even able to fit in a couple evenings of skiing under the stars with floodlights to light the trails and personal headlamps for better viewing. Every minute together was special to Alex. But he still had not told Natalie his true identity. A secret that had gone on for too long.

It was time to tell the truth and pray for the best. His parents would arrive in two days. In three days, the Gala Christmas Fashion show happened. Would his parents bristle at the idea of his dating someone below their social class even though she had a master's degree? Would Natalie forgive him for lying about who he was and his real position in the company?

He'd told Natalie they were going to someplace special for lunch, but he neglected to make reservations .With snow in the right pack and the holidays in play, many visitors had crowded the town and wanted lunch. He had no luck in getting a lunch time slot, but hoped his uncle had the right connections to make it happen, so he walked over and tapped on his open office door. "Got a minute, Sir William?"

"Sure, come in."

Sitting at the edge of the chair facing his uncle, he cleared his throat." I was wondering if you could help me get a lunch reservation for 1:00 today off the premises. It's quite important."

"What's this about? Are you breaking up a relationship and don't want it seen in the store?"

Alex shook his head. "No, quite the opposite. Or at least I hope it will be." He slumped back in the chair and began rubbing his great grandfather's ring with his thumb. "The lunch date is with someone special. She works here"

Sir William's eyes narrowed. "What's going on? You seem quite anxious."

"Well… when we first met she thought I was just one of the regular staff here, not management."

"How did that happen?"

Alexander grimaced. "Because I told her I was a personal shopper. I like that she considered me just another average male. Not someone who'd buy her expensive gifts and grant her every wish like so many in our social circle expect."

"And she doesn't know that we're related either, correct?"

"No, she doesn't. I said my surname was White. Didn't want her figuring out any family connections with our names. Today I want to tell her my real name and that my parents will be arriving soon. I don't want to overwhelm her too much all at once. I want her to meet Emma tonight as a start."

"You haven't even introduced her to Emma? Really kept her in the dark. How do you think she'll respond when she hears the truth?"

Alexander raked a hand through his hair. "Honestly? I don't know. I hope she'll understand. If she doesn't, then I won't have to overcome my parents' objections to her social status even though she has a master's degree."

"Ah, yes. My sister is quite class conscious. She needs to understand that we're not judged by our family's lineage in America. Merit and skills are what's important. I didn't hire you because of our family's pedigree. I hired you for your skills and brain."

"So can you get me a lunch reservation at a good table to make our talk a little easier?"

"Let me see if I can get you in at Viva Tapas. It's steps from the store and I'm a good friend of the manager. He can always find a spot for me. He usually holds a spare table or two for special guests even when they're full."

While his uncle made the phone call, Alexander's thoughts returned to Natalie. Once again he began rubbing his great grandfather's ring. *Shouldn't have waited this long. Hope this doesn't backfire on me. I'm the same guy she's known all along. Only now she'll know I've got substantially more euros in my bank account than she expected.*

The sound of his uncle slapping his hands together caused his attention to pivot back to Sir William. "How did the call go?"

"It's always good to talk to Victor. Always has something funny to say that lifts my spirits. You're in luck. There's one of his special tables available that's off to the side for celebrities who want to have a quiet lunch. The reservation is under your name. Tell whoever is at the front podium that Victor arranged a table for you."

Both men stood and Alexander shook his uncle's hand. "Thanks for getting the reservation. Say a few prayers that I'll say the right words at lunch."

Sir William walked with Alexander to the door. "Step away from the office for a bit. Give yourself some time to think. Walk me down to "Bites." My legs need some exercise. What are your plans for a place to live? You don't want the hotel to be your regular residence, do you?"

"I've already been checking the Internet for apartments and condos. While it's nice to have the hotel's kitchen available for whatever I need from room service, I'd like to have little more space to relax and unwind."

"Properties are snatched up quickly during our busy season. It may take a while to find something. I can recommend you to an agent who has a good pulse on the market and can get showings for her preferred clients before they hit the public market."

Their conversation continued as they rode the elevator down to the first floor and for their walk to the restaurant. Alexander was so engrossed in their conversation about his future with Rothwell's and living in Aspen that he failed to notice Natalie's roommate filling a sales rack with dresses just a few feet away from him.

But Laura noticed him and the friendly banter he was having with the store's owner as if they were old friends. She finished stocking the rack and decided to take a hasty break, It was time to make a quick retreat to the employees locker room. Once there, she grabbed her phone from her locker she texted Natalie.

> **Laura:** Saw Alex walking through the  store with Rothwell like old friends. Something's going on.

> **Natalie:** Think he's spying on us and reporting back to the boss?

> **Laura:** Time for you to find out. I don't want to lose this job and neither do you. Find out what his game is. .

# Chapter 12

## Telling Natalie the Truth

Alex and Natalie had arranged a meeting point at the store's main doors leading out to the street to go to lunch. Since he arrived early, he used the time to buy Natalie a deep green cashmere and silk scarf with flecks of gold running through it. Without glancing at the sales tag, he gave the clerk his credit card. "This is a gift for a special lady."

"It's an excellent choice, sir. I'm sure she'll love it," the sales clerk replied . She removed the tag, wrapped the scarf in tissue paper, and placed it in a glimmering Rothwell's shopping bag.

He stood by the door and only had a short wait until he saw Natalie heading toward him giving him a big smile. His heart thumped a heavy rhythm as he strode to meet her.

Natalie wrapped her arm around his elbow when they met. "Have you been waiting long?"

"I was here a bit early, but I made good use of my time to buy you something. Consider it an early gift to celebrate the upcoming fashion show that I know will be a success."

Her eyes danced with delight as she pulled out the scarf. "It's lovely. Thanks for thinking of me."

"Let me put it on you." As he gently wrapped the scarf around her neck, they gazed at each other as if nothing else in the world mattered. Alex leaned in for a kiss but was jostled as a shopper accidentally bumped into them. He sighed and wrapped his arm around Natalie. "Looks like we're in the way."

Natalie nodded. "Let's go eat. I'm famished. Where are we going?"

"I've got a reservation at Viva Tapas. It's around the corner. Their express lunch combos are guaranteed to be ready in 15 minutes."

Opening the door to the restaurant, their senses were hit with the aromatic blend of garlic, rosemary, and oregano mixed with the sizzle of meat on the grill. The restaurant was packed with diners enjoying their meal and their chatter overwhelmed the sound of the background instrumental tango music. The lobby was full as well with people waiting to be seated.

Natalie whispered in Alex's ear. "Glad you have a reservation. Looks like a long wait."

"Stay here while I make my way through the crowd to the host podium."

"Fine. I'll check my messages."

Alex nodded and she moved to the side to wait. Her first text was from Laura, which she read through twice. *How strange? Why would the store owner and Alex act like they were old friends? He started working there only a few weeks ago like me.*

Her hands trembled as she pulled off the scarf and checked the label. Simone Darroze. One of the designers being featured in the Christmas fashion show. Though she didn't remember the prices of her clothing line, she knew all the dresses featured in the show were priced over $5,000.

From the feel of the scarf it was probably cashmere, which would be pricey. Yet Alex called it a little something. How could he afford it on a personal shopper's salary? *He's definitely hiding something and I'm going to find out what it is. I've got to know what he's hiding from me.*

She turned back toward the front podium and saw Alex waving to her. She put on a big smile and joined him as they were escorted to a table on the far side of the dining room in a small alcove. The host pulled out her chair and laid a napkin in her lap once she sat.

Before they could start a conversation, their server appeared. "What drinks may I start you with?"

"Earl Grey tea for me," Natalie replied.

"I'd like a large bottle of Perrier. And we'd like to order the express lunch now. Natalie, how does the charcuterie platter sound with an order of empanadas?"

"Sounds like something quick and easy to eat. Let's do it."

Once the server left, Alex reached for Natalie's hands and smiled. "Glad we could get away from the store for a while. There's something I want to discuss with you. I won't be able to cheer for you from the sidelines at the fashion show…" He hesitated and held a tight smile.

Natalie held her breath as her heart sunk to the floor. *Is he breaking up with me in the restaurant? Was that scarf a goodbye gift?*

"You see… my parents and I are invited guests for the fashion show. They're coming into town to spend time with me and my sister. Plus Mummy loves fashion shows so it's a win-win for her."

Natalie sputtered, "How… why… are you invited guests? The show only supplies tickets for the event to their best customers and celebrities."

"My family can easily afford it. My full name is Alexander Davies-White. Daddy is a member of the LSE, that's the London Stock Exchange, as was my grandfather."

"But you said you were a personal shopper for the store? Why did you lie to me?"

"I was fascinated with you the moment we met. I wanted to spend more time with you than just those few minutes making an exchange. I didn't want you to think of me as another rich guy.

Being a personal shopper would put us more at an even level. I loved that you thought of me as an average person. It was refreshing. I can't tell you the number of times women have come on to me because they considered me a blank check to fulfill all their monetary wishes."

Natalie pulled her hands away and glared at him. "But you kept on playing your game. You couldn't trust me? You were so afraid that I was a gold digger?"

Alex sputtered. "No, not at all. As a fellow worker, you treated me with respect."

"Did you just buy that first scarf to lure me into your fantasy relationship? And now you've given me another one? Is this all just a game to you?"

"No, The return was for my sister. Please you're taking this all the wrong way."

"Really? You've never even mentioned you had a sister. How many times have you lied to me? The whole Thanksgiving thing was a lie. I was such a fool to believe you."

"I wanted to give you and Laura a special treat."

Natalie's nostrils flared has she rubbed her hands on her legs as if not wanting to let them come near his hands on the table. "Did you and Cade have a good laugh?"

Alex lowered his gaze and folded his hands on the table while constantly rubbing his grandfather's ring. "No it's not like that. I'm staying at the hotel. Cade has been handling my personal requests for reservations just like he would do for any other guest."

"Did you even go to the same college? Or was that a lie as well?"

Alex reached his hand across the table praying that Natalie would take it and try to understand. "That part is true. We discovered our common background in one of our early conversations."

Natalie leaned back in her chair then threw her arms across her chest and blew out a deep breath. "You could be honest with the hotel concierge, but you couldn't be honest when we met or during our many times together. You really are a piece of work.

Unlike you, I have to work for a living. I've lost my appetite. I'm going back to my job. At least that's real." She pushed back her chair, threw her napkin on the table, then turned swiftly away to leave the restaurant.

Alex slumped into his chair letting his hands hang limply off the armrests as his eyes stared at the ceiling unseeing. *I can't believe this happened. How in the world did trying to tell Natalie the truth turn out so badly? Didn't even get the chance to tell her how much I wanted her to meet my parents.*

*Dear God, help me fix this mess I've made. I don't want to lose Natalie. I've never met anyone like her. She's very special to me. I've fallen for her and want to make this work.*

# Chapter 13

## Alexander and Emma

After the restaurant debacle, Alexander returned to the store. Since there was no longer any reason for him to be concerned about anyone seeing him use the private elevator, he marched directly to it. He breezed past the receptionist and gave a brief wave. "Only here for a couple of minutes to get some paperwork." He hastily picked up some files and called Cade. Not in the mood for any bantering, his voice was gruff. "Hope there's a limo to pick me up at the store a.s.a.p. to take me to the hotel"

There was silence on the other end of the line for a moment. "Uh, yes, sir. Just sent one over. I'll let the driver know to look for you. Anything else I can help you with? Sounds like you're having a bad day."

"You can definitely say that. But I don't want to talk about it. Have you seen my sister recently?"

"I believe so. I heard her mirthful laugh that seems to dance in the air in the lobby. By the sound of it, I'd say she was heading to the elevators."

"Good, now make that call." He disconnected the call and bounded back through the office without even nodding to the receptionist as he left. Going down the elevator he had the urge to seek out Natalie and smooth things over with her, but this was probably not the right time or place. Once the elevator doors opened, he looked straight ahead and made a beeline for the exit.

While he waited for his ride, he sent Emma a text...

> **Alex:** Have some free time? Need to talk. Get some advice. Heading to hotel now.

Emma's text reply came in minutes. A smile started to form at the edge of his mouth with her positive response, but it fell quickly. He gazed aimlessly out the window alternately tapping his hands on his knees. "Need to make this better," he mumbled under his breath.

After what seemed to be eternity, he arrived at the hotel. Without waiting for the driver to open the door, he leaped out of the car and dropped a tip in the surprised driver's hand. When he entered the lobby, he noticed Cade was assisting someone, so he dropped a short text to him to apologize for his rude behavior. He considered the man his friend and didn't want to create any bad feelings between them due to his frustration with Natalie. Next he texted Emma.

> **Alex:** On the way to my room
> now. Meet me there.

Emma wasn't in his suite when he got there. He strode to the mini bar and pulled out a bottle of Perrier, took a sip and flopped into the nearby leather chair. He rubbed his family ring again as his thoughts jumbled in his head. A long ten minutes later, he heard a knock on the door in the tapping pattern of his sister. He bolted from the chair and flung the door open. "It took you long enough, come in."

Emma leaned against the door frame and crossed her arms over her chest. "You know I don't live at your beck and call. If you can't treat me more civilly I'll just leave."

Alexander raised his hands in a conciliatory gesture. "Yes, I know. You're here as a favor to me. Forgive my bad manners."

Emma smiled and sauntered into the room. "That's much better. Tell me. What's the big emergency? Did Uncle Will fire you?"

"Hah. Fire me. Never going to happen. We're on the same wavelength. I thought it was the same with Natalie."

"What happened?"

He squeezed her hand as she sat in a chair that was angled to face him. "It started out fine. I gave her a beautiful scarf as a celebration for her upcoming fashion show as we left the store. After we ordered our lunch at Viva Tapas, things somehow went haywire."

"What did you say to her?"

"I told her our family were invited guests for the fashion show and I'd be spending time with them rather than be with her backstage."

84

Emma sputtered. "You said that? That sounds like a kiss off with the scarf as a farewell gift. What exactly have you been telling her about who you are?"

"I let her know how much I liked being with her but kept my identity a secret."

"For six weeks you've strung her along, not telling her about the family or Uncle Will?"

He nodded his head sheepishly. "Yes I wanted to keep it on a friendly note until I felt we had something to build on as a relationship."

"But you were building on a relationship full of lies." She pulled both of his hands into hers. "Alexander, my dear sweet brother, you can't chart a relationship on a graph and give it numerical values. That only works with business forecasting. Even then glitches can happen."

He glared at her. "How can you say I did something like that?"

"Because you've done that several times with past girlfriends. You analyze your relationships as to how they will add to the bottom line of your life's expectations."

Alexander slumped back in his chair and gazed at the ceiling. Could Emma really be right? His mind wandered over past relationships and realized he often looked at them like balance sheets. By not telling Natalie the truth about his identity, he was keeping her at arm's length. She on the other hand openly shared her hopes, dreams, and even insecurities in reaching her goals. "So, what do I do now?"

Emma chuckled. "That's easy. Turn on the Alexander charm. Shower her with gifts that would have meaning to her."

"The way she rebuffed me about the scarf. I don't know if that can work."

If you really want her in your life in a big way, I'll help make it happen."

"Yes. Please help me."

Emma walked over to the desk, opened the drawer, pulled out several of the hotel stationery sheets, and laid them on the desk. "I want you to write down all the things you like about Natalie, favorite memories together, her favorite drinks, snacks, and anything else that's significant to the two of you."

"How's that going to help? Do you want to remind me of what I've lost?"

"Just do it. You'll see. What's Uncle Will's receptionist's name?"

"Gwen Glover."

"Right. I'm never good at names." Emma punched in the number for Uncle Will's office on her phone and waited for the call to be picked up.

"Good afternoon, Rothwell's how may I assist you?"

"Hello Gwen, this is Emma Davis-White. Is my uncle, Sir William, in?"

"No, I'm sorry he isn't. Can I take a message? Or do you want to leave one on his voice mail?"

"Maybe you can help me. I talked to him about doing something special for one of the employees, Natalie Baynton. She's co-chairing the Christmas fashion show and has personally helped me pick out something for Uncle Will's big party. If I wanted to send a little thank you to her, where would I send it? I don't want the delivery person scouring the store to find her."

"How sweet of you. Let me check with Sheryl Carballo and see where she's scheduled to be. Please hold for a minute…Thanks for holding. Ms. Bayton is in the private events room for V.I.P. fashion shows on the second floor behind the evening gowns. It's the door on the left behind the registers in that section."

"Great. Can you let the sales clerk know someone will be dropping by and needs access to the room?"

"Certainly."

"I can see why my uncle calls you a true gem. Thank you for your help." Emma clapped her hands after hanging up the phone. She walked over to the desk where Alexander was writing fervently. "Good. You have a number of ways you can show her you really care with these notes. Start by sending her a light snack of her favorites and apologize for ruining her lunch and asking for her forgiveness. And then we can work on the other ideas to win her back."

# Chapter 14

## Winning Over Natalie

When Natalie escaped from the restaurant, she stomped down the street for a few minutes trying to ease her anger. Laura wasn't available to vent her feelings as she'd be in fittings for the rest of the day. Once she calmed down, she returned to the store. With no more time left for lunch, she picked up some peanut butter crackers from the vending machine in the employees' lounge and devoured them with haste before going back to the V.I.P. room.

She focused all her thoughts on putting the dresses together in the order they would be worn on the racks. She flinched when there was a knock on the door. Sheryl, her boss, would have walked right in. When she opened the door, she was surprised to see a server from "Bites" holding a paper bag.

"I have a delivery for Natalie Baynton."

"That's me, but I didn't order anything from the restaurant."

The server handed the bag to her. "I don't know who ordered it. I was told to deliver a chicken pesto wrap, no mayo, with Earl Grey tea."

Natalie took the bag." I'm sorry I don't have a purse for a tip."

The server grinned. "Not a problem. A generous tip was included in the payment. Enjoy your meal."

As the server left, Natalie looked into the bag and saw an envelope with the food. The note inside It read…

*Natalie,*

*I enjoyed our first meal together and sharing our likes and dislikes. You are definitely one of my faves. That lunch date made me want to spend more time with you. I deeply regret not telling you the truth earlier on. I've enjoyed the way we fit together and don't want anything*

*to spoil it. And yet I have. Please give me*
*a second chance to explain.*
*Hopefully, Alex*

Natalie caught her breath, "He remembered what I ordered. And he even included extra napkins and a mini hand sanitizer, so I don't stain the dresses." She started putting the bag and its contents off to the side, but then her stomach grumbled. *I'll just eat a few bites and sip some tea. It doesn't mean I've forgiven him. It's probably better this way anyhow. This is just another reminder to concentrate on my career. My full focus has to be on this fashion show to prove my value to Rothwell's.*

Yet as she worked her thoughts kept drifting back to Alex. She had looked forward to seeing him each time they were together. It felt so special. But could she trust him again? It was too confusing.

Ninety minutes later, another knock came from the door. This time it was a sales clerk from the evening gowns department carrying a long slim gift bag.

"This just came. Are you celebrating a special event today?"

Natalie smirked. Storming out of a restaurant and leaving a so-called boyfriend behind was not an event she would celebrate. She took the bag.

"Well someone thinks it is."

As the clerk turned and walked away, Natalie pulled out the single long stemmed red rose with a spray of baby's breath that was held in an elegant crystal vase. The note inside read…

> *Natalie,*
> *This rose's beauty is a perfect match for yours.*
> *Give me the time to make it up to you for the*
> *wrong I've done.*
> *Optimistically, Alex*

Natalie shook her head and sighed, *What am I supposed to do with you, Alex? How can you be so sweet to me when you've been lying to me for weeks? I can't do this. I can't be involved with someone now.* She picked up the vase and placed it on a display table 10 feet away. It was out of her way but not out of her sight. She returned to her work once again and did her best to try to push thoughts of Alex out of her mind, but it was fruitless.

As she was finishing her work for the day, the door opened and Sheryl Carballo walked in with another fashionably dressed woman.

"How's everything going, Natalie?" Sheryl asked.

"Good. All is ready for a run through tomorrow."

"Fantastic. This is one of our VIP clients I'm allowing to get a sneak peek of the gowns so she can pick up something special for Sir Williams' Christmas ball. Show her what we have and anything else that she would like to see. Please make sure you can schedule her for a fitting before the ball as needed. When you're finished lock up and go home."

The woman smiled at Natalie and extended her hand. "I've heard good things about what you're doing with the show. I know you want to get home and relax, so let's not waste any time. Show me the dazzling line up."

"It's my pleasure. I know you're sure to find something to your liking in our special holiday collection. Follow me, please." Natalie walked to the racks of clothes in individual cloth bags and wondered who this woman was. She didn't recognize her as a celebrity, but there was something familiar about her. "What styles do you like? Slim and sleek? Shimmering? Soft and flowing?"

"I'll put myself in your hands. Pick out what you think will make me look best and stand out in a good way at the ball. Let me take off my coat and we can get started."

Natalie assisted the woman in taking off her oversized faux fur coat and placed it on a hanger while the woman placed her leather hobo bag on the nearby chair. "Well, I can see you appreciate the Saint-Laurent style by your bag and coat. Do you want to stay with that line or look at others?"

"You know your designers. I'm not strictly Saint-Laurent. I'm open to other names."

As they sorted through a number of dresses, Natalie got a better feel for her likes and dislikes in clothing styles. They chatted easily about current fashion trends and the goings on in Aspen. It only took 30 minutes to narrow down the choices to one special dress.

"This one is perfect. It makes just the right statement." Natalie picked up her tablet and was getting ready to ask for the woman's name and number to set up the fitting, but the woman spoke first.

"Thank you for your time. I can see you are an asset to Rothwell's. Do you plan on making your career here or would you prefer to start a clothing store of your own?"

That was an easy one for Natalie to answer. In the few short weeks she'd been there she'd fallen in love with the Rothwell style. She couldn't imagine working anywhere else. It was where she had met Alex, and they became friends and started to be something more. But she shouldn't be thinking about him. "Yes, I want a career with Rothwell's."

"That's good to know. I think the store is pretty special as well. Now I know you're going to ask me for my name and contact info for my fitting. I'll give that to you in a minute. First, I have something for you." She reached into her bag and pulled out a small glittering Rothwell's gift bag and handed it to Natalie. This is from Alexander. He's my brother. My name is Emma Davies-White."

Natalie stretched out her hand to give it back, but Emma waved it away. "Hear me out. Like many men, my brother can sometimes act like an idiot, which he did by withholding who he was. When you're wealthy, many people will try to latch on to you for what they can get out of the relationship. We don't want to be liked for our money, but for who we are. That's what Alexander loved about being with you. He is quite brilliant with numbers, statistics, and reports, but he doesn't always know the best way to phrase things. When he told you we were invited guests to the fashion show, it wasn't what you would call a brush off. He said that because he wanted our parents to meet you after the show."

Natalie stared dumbfounded. "But he looked so smug when he said it."

Emma rolled her eyes. "Whenever he wants to share a secret, he gets that look of I know something you don't. But there was nothing smug about it. If he wants to introduce you to Mummy and Daddy, you're someone special to him."

Natalie's eyes, which a moment ago were hooded, now gleamed with joy. "For real? You mean that?"

"Yes. Now open the bag. I'm dying to know what he bought. And ready to explain if it makes no sense to you."

Natalie cautiously pulled away the tissue paper and brought out a square velvet jewelry box. Inside was a gold charm bracelet. She ran her finger over each of the charms. They consisted of a shooting star Heart, red glass heart with a golden arrow going through it, shopping bag, dress on a hanger, and a love letter envelope. As her eyes welled up, she said, "It's beautiful."

"Yes, he chose well. Now it's time to leave. There's a limo waiting for you. Alexander won't be in it. He's in the lobby at your dorm hotel. You'll need to let him know if you're willing to talk in person. He's truly a fine man. Give him another chance."

Natalie picked up the flower vase and tucked the bracelet back into the gift bag. "Okay, I'd like to talk to him. I'll lock up and get my coat from the employee's lounge."

Once they locked the door behind them and entered the public part of the store, Emma gave Natalie's shoulder a quick squeeze. "Give him the time he needs to explain everything. Don't jump in too early if he flubs up again. There's more he wants and needs to tell you. I think the two of you make a great couple."

"Thanks. I'm glad we had the chance to talk." Natalie turned and walked toward the elevator and took it to the first floor. Her thoughts returned to what Emma had said about Alex. She hadn't absolved him for his lying, but Emma gave a reasonable explanation as to why he did it. And she realized she hadn't given him a chance to explain at all. *Why did I jump to the wrong conclusions so quickly? He's not like my ex-boyfriend. I know I need to focus on my job. Can't I do both -- have a relationship and my career?*

Exiting the elevator, Natalie rushed towards the employee lounge, picked up her phone and texted Alex...

**Natalie:** Yes let's talk. This time I won't interrupt you. See you soon.

# Chapter 15

## *Natalie and Alex*

The limo driver got out of the car and opened the back door for Natalie as she walked to the curb.

"Good evening Miss Baynton, there's an assortment of hot and cold beverages in the middle cabinet. Relax and enjoy whatever you choose."

Natalie slipped into the back seat and perused her options, choosing a hot cocoa. She flipped down a small table on the half wall in front of her.. As she sipped the warm drink and watched the passing view, a smile began to form on her face. *Falling for someone was not a part of my career goals. Guess I miscalculated on how to handle my feelings.*

She shook her head and chuckled to herself remembering Proverbs 16:9. We can make our plans, but the Lord determines our steps. Closing her eyes, she silently prayed. "Lord, is there a future for Alex and me as a couple? He's trying to make amends. And I need to ask his forgiveness for jumping to the wrong conclusion about him. We seem a fit with how easy conversation flows between us. I enjoy his playful side, love of statistics, and his interest in my work. He treats me as an equal. Please let me see if this is in your plans for me."

As she opened her eyes, she realized they were almost back at her dorm hotel. Butterflies began to dance about her stomach. When they turned the corner and into the drive for the front door, Alex walked out and pointed to a bunch of small signs stuck into the snowy front lawn. They read. *Proverbs 31:25. She is clothed with strength and dignity; she can laugh at the days to come! You're the one for me.*

Natalie threw her hands over her mouth and her eyes welled up. "I can't believe what I'm seeing. If that's not a sign, I don't know what is."

When the car stopped, Alex opened her door. Leaning his head inside, he gave her a tentative smile as one hand gripped the door frame while the other tugged at his wool coat. "Thanks, um, for agreeing to meet me." He tilted his head toward the sidewalk as he stammered. "It's a bit chilly outside. Not very conducive to walking and talking. I doubt there are any quiet spaces in the public areas of your place where we could talk...But, um, Rothwell's hotel has a restaurant with tables in small alcoves where you can dine and have private conversations. I made a reservation there, Tentative, of course, on what you wanted. I'll change it if you prefer to go somewhere else. This is your choice."

Natalie bit her lip and was silent for a moment as she clutched and unclutched her hands. She didn't want to be heartbroken again. That's why her career was her main focus. Should she risk a relationship with Alex after he deceived her? Would his parents even like her?

Then memories of their numerous conversations, the way he made her laugh, and how he made her feel special, flooded her mind. She timidly smiled and patted the seat beside her. "C'mon out of the cold. Let's go to the restaurant. We'll order drinks and appetizers and see where this goes."

Alex's eyes lit up as he slid into the seat beside her and closed the door.

His hand reached over and brushed against her fingertips uncertain if she might reject the touch of his hand.

He broke the awkward silence and grinned. "Was my sister able to find a dress she liked? Sometimes she can be ultra picky."

Natalie let out the breath she'd been holding in. "Not at all. She has a good eye for fashion and knows what works best for her. The hard part was narrowing it down to one dress to wear to the charity ball."

"Since you've been the one deciding on the dresses for the show, are there any that you'd like to wear?"

Natalie smirked and shook her head. "No way. That would be an alternate reality. I'm not a model and I have no need to wear one of them."

Alex raised an eyebrow. "Surely you've had one of those Cinderella moments where you were magically dressed in a ball gown that would catch the Prince's eyes. What would you be wearing?"

"Of course, I've considered a Cinderella dress. It's changed over the years. Now it would be a royal blue to midnight blue. It would have sequins, lace appliques, a tulle skirt, but not too wide of a skirt."

"Is there anything like that at the store?"

"There's one or two that could work, but I don't need to fulfill a little girl's fantasy anymore." She glanced out the window lost in thought for a moment and pointed. "Look we're here already."

When they got out of the car, Alex reached out his hand. "Would it be all right if I held your hand?"

Natalie nodded and cautiously slipped her hand in his.

There was an awkward silence as they walked through the lobby. Alex cleared his throat and turned to Natalie. "We're not going to the main restaurant like we did for Thanksgiving. This is one of the smaller ones reserved just for suite guests. It has a limited menu but I'm sure we'll find something that works."

The restaurant was designed to give the appearance of a manor house's study or library, but without the books. The floors were a polished teak and each table was flanked with a plush 6-foot high semi-circle banquette which gave them the option to sit side by side in the center or across from each other. They chose to sit across from one another.

After their server took their order, Alex unconsciously rubbed his finger around his grandfather's ring and timidly smiled. "Did you know that fifty-six percent of Americans believe in love at first sight? I don't know if what I felt was love at first sight. I only knew I wanted to learn more about you. What inspires you? What makes you happy? And I

103

wanted to share those experiences with you. Telling you I worked at the store gave us common ground. Statistics show that sixty-five percent of those people who began a workplace romance did so because they shared a commonality."

Alex broke eye contact with Natalie and looked down. "And, um, I'm not exactly working for the company as yet, but I have been reviewing reports and analyzing data on how the company is run." He raised his eyes to meet hers. "I'm officially starting January 1. The announcement will be made at the charity ball."

Natalie frowned. "What do you mean? I know it's not as a personal shopper."

"Not hardly." His eyes flickered with mirth. "You've probably noticed I have a penchant for numbers and statistics. I'll be taking over the reins as the store's financial controller."

"You're what?" Natalie's eyes grew wide. "So you're not a VIP guest, but head management."

Their server delivered their glasses of sparkling water with a twist of lime, which Natalie immediately picked up and drank.

"I know, Natalie, it's a lot to take in. I'm actually both. And there is something more."

Natalie gripped her glass with both hands and whispered, "Go on."

"Sir William is my uncle. I've been working with him for a few years at his other locations to assess how the business is run. The **United States has the largest apparel market of any country. Clothing and accessories account for over three hundred billion in sales. I want to help** Sir William tap into that market the best he can."

"Wow. I was not expecting that." Natalie slumped into the back of the banquette.

"You love fashion and style. I love my numbers and statistics. This is my dream job. You're working towards yours, and from what I've heard you're on that trajectory."

"You mean that, about my job?" Natalie's eyes brightened. She leaned forward and rested her arms on the table.

"Your enthusiasm about your work became evident the more I got to know you." Alex reached for her hands, but she didn't grasp his. "Can we start over? I want to continue sharing lunches with you. And spending time together outside of work. Give me a second chance."

"We're so different, Alex." Natalie's shoulders dropped. "I don't fit in your world. I didn't go to an exclusive university. Don't have the money to buy my favorite designer fashions. I've never even been out of the U.S."

"I don't care about any of that. We got along fine when you thought I was a personal shopper. I'm still the same person. We fit together then and still do."

"What about your parents? And Sir William? What will he think about us dating?"

"Uncle Will's main concern was that I treat you with respect and care. That's what I intend to do."

"And your parents?"

"Well, Mummy might be a bit of a stickler at first, but she loves talking about fashion. She'll come around. Both my parents love me and will be pleased I've have found someone to love who loves me in return."

Natalie's eyes began to mist. "You found someone you love. You really mean that?"

"Falling love wasn't in my plans, but you grabbed my heart with your smile. I think about you each day and can't wait to be with you again. Do you feel the same about me?

Natalie squeezed his hands tightly, as a grin spread across her face. "Yes. Falling in love was not in my plans either, but I'm ready to see where this goes."

"Me, too. But first there's the fashion show and meeting Mummy and Daddy. After that, everything else will seem easy."

"I pray that's the case. I'll admit I am a bit nervous about both events."

"I've got faith in you. You'll do fine." Then he winked. "I'll be cheering for you from the VIP seats."

# Chapter 16

## Prepping for the Fashion Show

When Natalie arrived at work the next morning, she had the urge to sing at the top of her lungs, "He loves me… he really loves me" as she waltzed through the store. She didn't actually waltz, but she did feel as giddy as Scrooge when he discovered he hadn't missed Christmas. It was a bright new day and even the blustering snow outside and the work ahead of her for the final countdown for the fashion show tonight couldn't steal the joy she felt.

While she strode through the store, she heard customers ooh and aah about Christmas gifts and heard snippets of conversation about the fashion show. Her mouth went dry. *Am I really ready for this? Even with Sheryl co-hosting with me? Lord help me stay calm and focused.*

The fashion show fitting room was abuzz with activity when Natalie entered. Sheryl was on her phone and reviewing paperwork at the same time. They gave each other a quick wave and Natalie pointed to where she was heading. She halted at a rack of two dresses and pursed her lips. *Yes, I'm still love these choices. Once Sheryl is free, I'll get her final approval on which to wear. Wonder if I'll get to wear jewelry on loan from the store like the models? Will have to see what Sheryl suggests.*

She moved to the podium she'd use tonight and perched on the stool before it. Flipping open the tablet there, she scrolled through the notes detailing the designer names plus jewelry and accessories for each model. After reviewing them multiple times, she closed the screen and blew out a deep breath. *I've got this. This is the career I want and will continue to work hard to make it happen.*

She jumped when she was tapped on the shoulder.

"A bit tense?" Sheryl asked as she pulled a chair next to Natalie.

"You could say that."

"Then let's take a break, get a snack and pick out our jewelry. They'll be delivered once the store is closed."

Even though Natalie could never afford the choices Sheryl suggested, she enjoyed the fantasy spree of choosing sparkling jewels to wear. That was followed by a show rehearsal making sure the dressers knew each of the items worn in the proper sequence.

Natalie felt emotionally drained when they finally finished the day's details at the store. The next step was moving everything to the grand ballroom at Rothwell's Hotel. She sent a text message to Alex.

> **Natalie:** Got a short break. Need to decompress. Want food. No distractions. Kick off shoes. Be with you. Suggestions?
>
> **Alex:** With family. In Sir Will's upstairs. Can break off. My suite? Living room. Table and chairs. Room service. Bedroom off limits!
>
> **Natalie:** Can you get a car to shuttle us?
>
> **Alex:** I'll check with Cade... Done. Car at front door in 5 minutes.

**Natalie:** I'll be there!

On the way to the hotel, Alex ordered a rush on room service for the two of them. Natalie felt a bit awkward going to his room but relaxed once they entered. His suite was on an upper floor and the living room window faced the ski slopes and mountains nearby. "What a spectacular view. My room view is the parking lot and another building."

"Uncle Will wanted to make sure guests had views worthy of their stay. Does the view help to decompress?"

"Yes, seeing the beauty of God's nature scenes always calms me. It's been a busy day and will stay that way until the show finishes."

"Let's move the table closer for the best view."

Soon after they rearranged the table, there was a knock on the door from room service.

The server put their food on the table. Once he left, Alex sat with Natalie. Holding hands, they closed their eyes and he prayed. "Heavenly Father, thank you for the wonderful blessings of our life and the food you set before us. Guide and direct Natalie today. Remove any anxieties she might be feeling. Fill her with joy as she runs through the show tonight. In Jesus name, Amen."

"Thanks for suggesting this, Alex. This protein bowl with quinoa, roasted veggies, avocado, and chicken breast tastes yummy. And the view tops it off. Your salmon and broccolini looks good as well."

"It tastes great, too. Did you know there were over 5 million hotel rooms in the United states and that 25% of their revenue comes from food and beverages. So by eating in the room we're helping improve Uncle Will's bottom line.

Natalie twirled her fork in her bowl and grinned. "You are certainly a fount of information."

Alex looked at the exterior view and pondered for a minute. "The hotel has wonderful massages to help you relax. Or I could give you a personal foot massage after you finish your meal."

"You'd do that for me?"

"You're going to be on your feet a lot today. They could use some refreshing."

After lunch, Natalie slipped out of her shoes, laid on the couch and propped her feet on a small pillow on Alex's lap. As they chatted, Alex gently rubbed her toes, feet, and ankles. Feeling the tension slip away, Natalie relaxed and soon drifted off to sleep. Alex slipped off the couch and set his phone's timer to 15 minutes. Then he sat in a nearby chair and stared lovingly at Natalie.

When the musical notes of the alarm sounded, Natalie's eyes popped open. "Oh no, how long have I been sleeping?"

"No worries. Only 15 minutes since you dozed. Do a quick freshen up and I'll walk you down to the ballroom. Then I'll be returning to the store to meet up with the family again.

# Chapter 17

## The Fashion Show

The upbeat music began as the thick silver curtain that separated the back of the stage from the audience opened to just the width of the runway leading down toward the guests seated. That was Natalie's cue to walk toward the podium..

"Good evening honored guests. It's our pleasure to welcome you to this annual Christmas fashion festival. Everything you see from clothes, to jewelry, and accessories are  available at Rothwell's and can be perfectly tailored to your size. Without further ado, let's see the clothes you'll want for the holiday season and beyond."

As the first model came out, butterflies raced around Natalie's stomach as if they were doing an Indie 500, but she smiled, maintaining her composure. Her words flowed smoothly, as she provided a running commentary of the model's attire.

After Natalie finished her segment, Sheryl switched places with her. Backstage, Natalie peeked through the curtains to see the guests' reactions. Her spirit brightened noting heads leaning together with pleased expressions and pointing to the models as they did their strut.

At the end of the show, Natalie joined Sheryl at the front of the stage as all the models did a final walk through and stood in front of the curtain. Once Sheryl thanked everyone for coming, there was a resounding applause.

While the models left the stage to change out of their clothes, Natalie and Sheryl stepped down from the stage to join the audience. Off to the side, Natalie caught a glimpse of Alex waving as he walked toward her with his sister and a couple she expected were their parents. Once they reached her, Alex gave her a quick hug and a kiss on her cheek. Then he slipped his arm around her waist and extended his other arm. "Natalie, I'd like to introduce you to my parents,

Geoffrey and Judith Davies-White. Mummy and Daddy, this extraordinary woman who co-hosted this show is my girlfriend, Natalie Baynton."

Natalie's free hand grasped at her skirt as she plastered on a smile. "It's a pleasure to meet you both. I hope you enjoyed the show."

Judith Davies-White nodded. "It was quite brilliant. I especially liked the way the clothes were set off with such wonderful accessories.. They truly made me want to buy the complete ensemble."

Geoffrey Davies-White grinned and hugged his wife. "I have no doubt she'll buy more than one outfit. I can see how several would suit her well."

While the two men chatted, Judith turned her attention to Natalie. 'Where did you attend university, my dear? Was it University of Edinburgh or London College of Fashion? Both have excellent fashion and design programs."

"No, ma'am. All my studies have been in the United States. I haven't had the pleasure of traveling overseas."

"Then you completed your studies at Fashion Institute of Technology or perhaps Parsons School of Design?"

Natalie shrugged. "No, those schools were way out of my budget. All my schooling was done right here in Colorado. I started in junior college to save money and get my basic classes completed. Then I worked my way through my undergraduate degree and master's in fine arts."

"Is that so? Charming."

Natalie noticed a flicker of disdain that passed over Judith's face that was quickly masked with the pinch of a smile. Well, she had been warned.

Judith caught Sheryl's attention as she made her way through the crowd. They clasped hands when they met. "Another smashing event. Sir William is lucky to have you on his team."

Sheryl patted Natalie on the shoulder. "Most of the credit goes to Natalie for this one. I let her take charge to see what she could do."

"Of course, you were right by there to guide her," Judith added smugly.

"Not necessary. Natalie has an eye for style and trends. She's a shining star in the Rothwell's company. I see big things ahead for her."

Natalie beamed as she touched her hand to her heart. "Coming from you, Sheryl, that means a lot. You've been a great mentor for me in understanding the Rothwell's brand."

"It's been great seeing you again Judith," Sheryl added, "but there's a few more guests I'd like to say hello to before they leave. See you tomorrow Natalie."

As Geoffrey Davies-White moved away to chat with some other people, Alex's attention returned to Natalie and his mother. "Natalie did a grand job on the show. I don't know much about fashion, but I could tell the guests were excited about the clothes."

"Yes, dear it was lovely. What are your plans for tomorrow?"

Before Alex could respond, a man dressed in the Rothwell's store attire came up to them and said, "Pardon my interruption. Are you Natalie Baynton?"

"Yes, I am."

He handed an envelope to Natalie. "I've been instructed to give you this from Sir William Rothwell." Then he turned and walked away.

Natalie held the embossed envelope with the Rothwell's logo in her hand. "I wonder why he didn't come by himself?"

"That's just Sir William's way," Alex replied. "He loves the financial return on these shows, but he'd much rather be watching sports. I'd bet he's holed up somewhere watching the world darts championship with some of his cronies. Open the envelope. See what he has to say."

Natalie opened the envelope and read the message.

> *Thank you for your part making this holiday fashion show a success. Let's talk more about it tomorrow. Come to my office at 2:00. I've already informed Sheryl of our meeting.*
> *Sincerely,*
> *Sir William Rothwell*

Alex pulled Natalie closer to him and wiggled his eyebrows. "Maybe he wants to give you a bonus. I think you deserve it."

As Natalie turned to face him, she caught a glimpse of his mother's expression. It wasn't one of joy and congratulations. Instead, her eyes narrowed and then she raised her chin and walked away. That look gave her goosebumps, Those feelings were quickly swept away by the gentle kiss on her lips from Alex, which warmed her heart.

# Chapter 18

## Sir Williams office

When the doors opened to the executive offices floor, Natalie took in a deep breath, then whispered to Alex. "I'm glad you're with me."

Alex winked. "If I weren't, you would still be standing by the first floor elevator. Lucky you have me and the magic key card."

Natalie rolled her eyes and squeezed his hand. "Seriously, I've never met Sir William and I'm a bit anxious." Her eyes widened as they crossed over the marbled hallway to the mahogany double doors which displayed an impressive etched brass plate with the name Rothwell Enterprises.

"Just be yourself. Relax. He's not some ogre." Again he tapped the key card to gain access to the offices.

The reception area continued with the same marble flooring as was in the hallway. The walls were adorned with pictures of the St. Moritz store as well as this one and a couple of photographs by John Fielder, the premier photographer of Colorado landscapes. Leather club chairs and a polished tree trunk coffee table were on one side of the room and the other side had the reception desk with a wooden display case behind it.

Alex immediately walked over to the desk. "Good morning, Gwen. We're here to see Sir William."

"He's on a call. Once that clears, I'll let him know you're here."

To pass the time, Alex and Natalie gazed at the photos on the wall. Natalie pointed to a Fielder one. "I know right where he took that shot. He's really captured that scene."

The click of the office door opening, and Sir William's boisterous greeting stopped their conversation. "Didn't expect to see you Alexander."

"Well, you didn't give her a key card for the elevator, so how else was she to come up without my assistance?"

"Ah yes, I tend to forget that point at times. Come into my office. Let's chat." Rather than directing them two chairs in front of his impressive desk, he brought them to the sitting area which held four swivel chairs and a table in front of it which held an elegant china tea service. "Alex, would you do the honor of serving tea for us?"

"With pleasure, Sir William."

While Alexander poured the tea and added a tea biscuit on each saucer, Sir William leaned back in his chair. "I'm sure you're wondering why I asked you here, so we'll get right to it. As head of this corporation, I want it to be a work environment that is positive and self-affirming to everyone who works here. That means I have to take into consideration the effects of employee fraternization. By the way you look at Natalie, I see you care a lot about her. Natalie, is that caring feeling reciprocated? Or in any way is it bothersome to you?"

Natalie felt the heat rise on her face. "Sir William, I had no intention or desire to look for a boyfriend when I started work here." She reached for Alexander's hand. "Truth be told, we quickly began a friendship when we met as I considered him a fellow employee."

Alexander squeezed her hand. "Truly, there has been nothing untoward going on. We simply began to have lunch dates so we could talk."

Natalie smiled. "True. I had no idea Alex was related to you in any way until a couple of days ago."

"I knew I couldn't put it off any longer with my parents' arrival. I wanted them to meet her not just as the fashion show co-host but as my girlfriend. She also knows about my upcoming management position, and she pledged to keep it a secret until the formal announcement."

"Natalie, you understand that once he starts as CFO. he won't have the free time he has now."

Natalie beamed as she gazed at Alexander. "Like any other couple, we'll just have to find time together when we're off work."

"So this is more than a holiday crush?"

"Uncle Will, it's gone way beyond that." Alexander caressed Natalie's cheek. "Though we've only known each other for a short time, I've fallen in love with her."

Eyes glowing with joy, Natalie replied. "And I've fallen in love with him, too."

"Uncle Will, I know we come from different backgrounds, but I quite feel like we're a perfect match."

"Natalie, do you see Rothwell's as a stepping stone in your career or for the long term?"

"I love working with Sheryl. She challenges me to take on more tasks and grow into the position. I can only hope that when I can work into a position like hers and coach my staff as well as she does."

"Good to hear. Sales from last night were up twenty percent over last year. As a bonus, pick out something from the collection, or from the rack, that you'd like to wear to the charity ball."

Sir William turned toward Alex. "I assume she'll be your date?"

Natalie caught her breath. "That's so generous."

"You deserve it for all the hard work you did, but don't expect this to be a regular occurrence. I do, after all, have to run a business. I'm glad you're a part of it. I've already informed Sheryl about getting a dress as a bonus. Go, pick up something now."

Sir William walked with the two of them to the door and opened it. A movement on the far side of the reception area caught Alex's attention. "Mummy, what brings you to Uncle Will's office?"

Judith nonchalantly waved her hand. "Just trying to catch up with my brother."

Only Alex knew his mother better than that. *What was she up to?*

# Chapter 19

## Emma and Alexander

While Natalie went to pick out a dress, Alexander met his sister at "Bites." Once they gave their order to the server, Emma asked, "Your text was a bit cryptic. What is so urgent?"

"Mummy. She's up to something. She was lurking in Uncle Will's reception area when we finished our meeting."

How did your meeting go?"

Alexander's eyes brightened. "Quite well. In essence, he asked about our relationship if it was a short term thing. We assured him it was much more than that. It's so freeing to be open about our feelings for each other. I know we've only been dating a few short weeks, but I can't imagine being with anyone else. She's the first person I think of every morning and the last person I want to say goodnight to each evening."

"Sounds like you're quite smitten with Natalie." Emma raised her water glass. "My congratulations to you. Are you planning a special announcement over the holidays about the two of you?"

Alexander lowered his eyes and began rubbing his ring. "Well, statistically speaking the average American dates for about 2 1/2 years before planning an engagement. I don't think I could wait that long."

"Then don't. You're not the average American couple. First off, you're not even American. If what you feel is real, and you're willing to fully commit to the traditional marriage vows, then buy the ring. No marriage is going to be perfect. Look at Mummy and Daddy. They've had their trials."

"True. And back to Mummy. After the fashion show, she gushed more about what Sheryl had done and not Natalie. You know how status conscious she is. Do you think she would try to split us up and ask for Uncle Will's assistance in that?"

Emma rubbed her neck and frowned. "Hmmm, I know she's attempted that with some of my past relationships or tried to push me toward a more suitable match. But I will always make my own decisions."

Alexander leaned forward. "Can you have a chat with Mummy and see how she feels?"

Emma grinned like a Cheshire cat. "This might be the time I tell them about my secret life?"

"Oh really?" Alexander leaned back in his chair and tented his fingers under his chin. "What devious plans have you been holding back from me, dear sister?"

"Nothing you'd expect. But I think it would make Daddy happy. You know I'm a wicked poker player and love analyzing the odds."

"Oh, yes. You know how to play your cards well. But you're not planning on becoming a professional gambler, are you?"

Emma laughed. "Not my style though I do love the game. You see, I've been re-evaluating my future since I received the second installment of my trust at age 30, I wanted to find a way to grow that money more than just with minimal interest. Create a money stream so it will last. I don't want to keep asking Mummy and Daddy for money.

I started working with Percy Atkinson, one of the stock traders in Daddy's company. He directed me to courses I could take and mentored me. I'm proud to say I've become quite adept at making money. Now I want to get my securities license and work as a stock broker."

"So you're more than just a pretty face and an avid shopper," Alexander smirked and then applauded silently. "Good for you. Do you plan on sharing that information with both of them anytime soon?"

"Yes, I'd like to tell them Christmas Eve when we're all together. I've invited Percy to come to the ball and stay for Christmas to back me up when I make my announcement. I rather think telling Daddy I want to be a stock broker would be the best Christmas present he could receive."

"Truly. Daddy will be over the moon that you're joining the family business. If you're bringing Percy, Mummy may shift her focus to you rather than me."

"What about a special announcement from you?"

"Still under consideration."

## Chapter 20

## Christmas Charity Ball

Natalie sat still as Laura applied the finishing touches to her makeup. She wanted to look her best for Alex's mother. She might not be upper class like Alex's family, but she had the intelligence and wit to hold her own in any class. Alex assured her his mother would grow to love her as much as he did. A surge of happiness filled her with that thought.

"Don't smile when I'm putting on lipstick, even if you are thinking of Alex."

"Can't help it. Are you about done?"

"Let me set the makeup. A little hair touch up. Okay. Done. Take a lot of pictures at the party so I can live through your time there vicariously."

"I wish you were going, too."

Laura rolled her eyes. "It might be fun to dress up, but I do it more than enough as a model. Besides Cade is taking me to the movies. I've convinced him to see a rom-com Christmas movie."

"You've gone out with him a few times now. Is a romance brewing?"

"Not yet. Enjoying the friendship. But who knows."

Natalie's phone buzzed. "It's a text from Alex. They just arrived and he's coming up. Let's pray a quick prayer that I make a good impression with his parents, especially since we're sharing a limo with them."

They held hands and closed their eyes as Laura prayed. "Heavenly Father, fill Natalie with your peace and joy. Let her know that she is always tops in your heart. Make this evening a time of fun. May the donations overflow to greatly benefit the charities designated. Amen."

Soon a knock came at their door. Laura opened it and moved to the side so she wouldn't block his view of Natalie.

Alex's eyes widened and his mouth dropped open as he stood looking at her. "Natalie, I've always thought you were beautiful, but now you look even more stunning. A princess in full royal regalia would pale compared to the beauty that shines through you right now."

A symphony of joy filled her as she walked toward him. In this dress and the way Laura had prepared her makeup and hair, she felt like a princess. "You look quite elegant in your tux as well."

"Shoo," Laura said with a laugh. "Do your dreamy-eyed stuff in the car. Get out of here, so I can get ready for my date."

The car ride to Sir Williams' estate was filled with pleasant conversation. Alex's mother seemed impressed by her appearance. There was pleasant small talk with no snide remarks. Natalie had reviewed internet pictures of the estate, but it was even more impressive in person. After gaining entrance through the guard house  and massive iron gates, the drive curved through clusters of fir trees until they reached the massive stone and wood structure that was ablaze with lights. Though the home didn't have turrets and towers she couldn't imagine a castle being more impressive than this.

Once they entered the home, Alex's parents were immediately drawn to friends waving to them. Alex and Natalie made their way through the crowds and several rooms until they found the band playing in the main ballroom. After sipping their drinks and tasting a few of the appetizers passed around by the catering staff, Alex asked Natalie to dance. Through the floor was crowded with other couples. as they held each other close and their hearts beat together, it seemed like no one else was there.

When the dancing ended, Sir William called Alex to the band's platform with him. Natalie beamed with delight and snapped a few pictures as Alex gave a short speech, which included a couple of statistics and a joke. Her heart beat joyfully as he returned to her. *This is a man I could spend my life with.* Her eyes blinked. *Where did that thought come from? It's way too soon to think like that.*

Alex put his arm around her waist once he reached her and whispered in her ear, "Let's get away from the crowds for a bit." He took her hand and wove through a few hallways and down stairs until they reached the solarium. Lights highlighted several parts of the backyard. A full moon and thousands of twinkling stars added their own beauty. Alex pulled her close to him as they gazed into the night. He whispered in her ear, "I don't know if I've ever felt any happier than I am with you right now."

He pulled her chin up and their eyes locked until he drew her into a kiss. At first their lips brushed lightly, almost afraid of opening a door to a passion that could consume them. Then they kissed again and again like waves gently ebbing the shoreline. When they finally pulled apart, Natalie leaned against his chest as their hearts beat together to a song of love.

# Chapter 21

## Christmas Day

The next week leading up to Christmas Day was non-stop work at the store. Natalie continued to fill orders from the fashion show and added additional tailors so that any dress alterations would be completed and delivered for the holiday events from Christmas to New Year's. As sales traffic surged, it was also her responsibility to fill the clothes racks as needed. Leisurely lunches between Natalie and Alex dwindled to fleeting text messages throughout the day. Their evenings were now spent in quaint restaurants or in the coziness of Alex's suite, sharing takeout and watching movies. Yet, for Natalie, these quiet, relaxed moments with

Alex were everything she needed, a comforting escape from the non-stop buzz of work at Rothwell's.

Since she had little time to shop in person, she scoured the Internet trying to find the perfect gift for Alex. Even though they agreed there would be only one gift given to each other, she was having trouble finding just the right one. *What can I give to a guy that can easily buy anything he wants and not have to worry about the costs? I don't have money to spend like that.*

The idea for the perfect gift came during one of their evening conversations. They had just finished their take-out meal in his suite and were putting its disposable packaging in the trash bin. As Alex completed the task, he said, "Did you know that the world wastes more than 2 billion tons of food every year? That's why I try to do minimal orders of food so there's no waste."

A light bulb blinked on in Natalie's head. *He loves statistics, facts, and trivia. A book like that would be fun to peruse together.* As soon as she returned to her dorm hotel, she went online and purchased the largest book she could find filled with fun facts and trivia. She smiled as she completed the order. Maybe when they had extra time in the coming year they could compete in some of the trivia nights at the local pubs. They'd probably do well as a team.

On Christmas Eve, when Rothwell's closed, an audible sigh of relief swept throughout the store. It had been a long day and Natalie was ready to go home and relax. Well wishes for a Merry Christmas were exchanged between staff members as they made their way out to cars or buses. While the bus drove to her destination, she texted Alex. Though they weren't together in person, she felt wrapped in his love as they chatted. Tomorrow they would have the whole day together. She'd been invited to his family's Christmas lunch at Sir William's estate. It seemed a bit daunting thinking of being the only outsider there for the day, but she knew Alex would be beside her for moral support.

Christmas morning, Alex picked her up with a limo and they drove to a nearby church that Natalie had been attending when work allowed. Today it was filled with people in their wintry best attire. Fresh pine garlands adorned the entrance and throughout the church as well. Christmas greetings were exchanged with several people as they made their way to their seats.

The service began with the traditional hymns of "Joy to the World" and "O Little Town of Bethlehem," which Natalie and Alex joined in singing with the congregation. As they listened to the sermon message, and held hands, Natalie's heartbeats were filled with happiness and joy. *Could he be the one I'm meant to be with for the rest of my life? We've only been together less than two months but the easy way we chat, laugh, and can enjoy a quiet silence together feels like I've known him much longer. Lord if this is the man you want for me, please give me that assurance.*

After they left the church, they headed to Sir William's estate. Today it would only be the immediate family for brunch. She bit her lip as her heart pounded. *Would his mother ignore her?*

As if sensing her anxiety, Alex wrapped his arm around her and whispered, "Nothing to worry about. I'm here with you."

Going through the gates during daylight showed off both the natural and man-made beauty of the estate. Through the pines, she could now see the additional outbuildings that consisted of a barn, horse stalls, and a massive one story building. She pointed and asked, "What's that?"

"That's the activity center. It houses snowmobiles, skis, and toboggins. For summer months he has a couple of ATVs. There's also a billiard table, foosball table, poker table and some old fashioned arcade machines. Guests will never be bored here. We'll have to come back and try those activities another time. Did you know that the family that plays together stays together?"

Natalie rolled her eyes. "You know the phrase actually is -- the family that prays together stays together."

"Sure, but I think if you take the time to have fun together *and* pray you'll build a solid relationship." His gaze locked into hers. "I'd like to build a solid relationship, wouldn't you?"

Warm tingles spread through her body as she nodded and continued to gaze at him.

The car stopped and broke their concentration but gave time for a quick kiss before they stepped from the car.

When they entered the house, the sounds of jazzy instrumental Christmas music followed them as they walked from one room to another. The housekeeper escorted them to the smaller dining and family room area where everyone would assemble for brunch. Smaller was relative as the two open spaces amounted to three times the size of the apartment she shared with Laura.

"There's coffee and English Breakfast tea on the sideboard plus cream and sugar. Would you like some Danish pastries or anything else?" The housekeeper asked.

They both shook their heads and she left. Leaning closer to Alex, Natalie whispered, "What types of food will be served for brunch? Will you need to coach me on using the right utensils, so I don't create a faux pas?"

He playfully tapped her nose. "No need to worry about an assortment of miscellaneous flatware. Would you like coffee or tea? It's not Earl Grey, but that's available if you prefer."

While he poured them both tea and handed a cup and saucer to Natalie, he added more details. "Though we call it brunch, this will actually be our Christmas supper. The buffet will have an assortment of starters such as pâtés, chilled prawns, preserves, cheese, and baguette slices. The mains will include a roast turkey, like at your Thanksgiving, but our vegetable choices include parsnips, braised red cabbage, brussels sprouts, and mashed potatoes. Desserts will include an English trifle, plum pudding, and a Buche de Noel. The most traditional is the plum pudding, which goes back centuries. That's what the Cratchits' had in Dickens' *A Christmas Carol.*"

"With all those options, this will be my last meal of the day. I won't need anything more. I'll do nibbles to make sure I can try a bit of everything."

Sir William bounded into the room with a boisterous, "Merry Christmas Day. Let's make this a grand one. I see you have tea. Would you like something stronger like a Bloody Mary, Mimosa, or Mulled Wine instead?"

"No, thank you, Sir William." Natalie replied.

"No, Uncle Will. I'm good with the tea."

"So you came separate from your parents?"

"Yes, we went to a Christmas service, then came straight here."

The door chimes sounded announcing another arrival. They were soon joined by Alex's parents, Emma, and Percy, who stopped and placed gifts under the tree in the family room first. After greetings all around and everyone getting their drinks, Sir William raised his glass in a toast, "To family and another great year in business. We thank the Lord for our many blessings. May he continue to bless and guide us through the coming years."

The housekeeper and cook began bringing out the appetizers and placing them on the buffet so everyone could make their own choices and then take seats at the table.

As they ate, amusing banter and family stories filled their conversations. Natalie kept a tight smile on her face as Alex's mother made eye contact and conversation with everyone but her. Her hand gripped her skirt watching Alex get caught up in the memories. Am I being oversensitive? She glanced over at his mother and noted a smug look on her face that was turned to a smile as she turned away. Natalie's attention turned to the food on her plate, but her appetite had disappeared. When the conversation centered between Alex's parents and Sir William. Alex whispered to her as he squeezed her hand. "I'm so happy you're here with me and my family. Hope we haven't bored you with our family stories."

Natalie lessened the grip on her skirt and feigned a slight laugh. "Not at all. I love learning more about you." Looking deep into his eyes she could see he was clueless as to his mother's indifference to her.

Sir William rose from his chair. "I believe we've all had our fill of this festive meal. Let's adjourn to the great room for after dinner drinks and presents."

Natalie whispered to Alex. "Were we supposed to bring gifts?"

"No, it's only the tradition between my parents and Uncle Will. But I noticed Emma brought something. Wonder what it could be?"

Everyone settled on the couches and chairs that faced an elegantly decorated tree with gold and red ornaments while Uncle Will and his parents exchanged gifts.

Next, Emma spoke. "Now it's my turn for gifting. Uncle Will, there's nothing you lack that I could give you. So, I'm giving you my undying love and gratitude for being such a great uncle." Then she moved toward him and wrapped him in a bear hug.

"My next gift is for Natalie. As my brother's girlfriend, you deserve to know a lot more of his growing up history." Emma picked up a large gift bag and handed it to her. This is a digital photo frame that I've filled with pictures from his messy young childhood and awkward teen years so you can better appreciate the man he's become."

Alex glared at his sister, but a hint of mirth twinkled in his eyes. "Are you trying to scare her away from me already?"

Emma kissed him on the forehead. "No, dear brother. I want her to grow to love you as much as I do. Now one more gift for Mummy and Daddy, which Percy helped put together." She placed a wrapped gift the size of a large shoebox on her father's lap.

"What's this?" he asked as he opened the box and found a sheaf of papers with what looked like a series of financial accounts.

"That's a series of stock and options trading I've been doing with Percy for the last two years. At first, he helped me make decisions on what to trade. I took numerous courses and did shadow trades on my own until I felt competent to run them for real."

"She has a great grasp on analytics, sir, and spotting trends." Percy added.

"Why are you showing me this?"

"Because I want to become a stockbroker in your company and trade not only for myself, but others as well. "

"But you've just been dabbling with your own money."

"Just dabbling? Let me give you an example of what I know. Last week I doubled my investment in a company with a diagonal debit spread. I sold a call option with an expiration date the Friday after earnings because earnings announcements cause the cost of options to spike and bought a call option five weeks out at the same strike." Emma hesitated a moment before continuing to make sure her father was listening.

He gave her a nod, so she continued.

"I picked a strike a little lower than the expected move. This trade cost $3.39 per contract, and I bought 15 contracts for $5,085. I sold these options less than 24 hours later for $10,170 for a profit of, you guessed it, $5085. This is possible because the options sold before earnings command a premium that evaporates after the earnings announcement. Selling a call option also provides protection to the downside that makes the trade profitable even if the price doesn't rise even if it drops some."

Geoffrey's mouth fell open. "My word, Emma, you do understand stocks. How long will it take you to study for the exam so you can pass?"

Percy beamed at Emma. "Sir, she's ready now. She's just waiting for your approval to schedule."

Emma crossed her arms over her chest and held her chin up high. "How's that for a Christmas present? You're getting the next stock broker in the family to carry on the family tradition."

Judith stood up and threw her arms around Emma. "That's a wonderful Christmas present. I'm so proud of you."

# Chapter 22

## *Alone Time for Alex and Natalie*

While his parents gushed over the news of Emma, Alex turned to Uncle Will. "Mind if I took Natalie to your library to go over these pictures without any snarky remarks from my sister?"

"Of course, Alexander. Go ahead."

In the library, the next room over, they sat side by side on a couch as Alex gave details of the pictures and events shown in the album. After several minutes he stopped and caressed her face. "These photos show my past, but I want to create a future with you. I love seeing the excitement in your eyes when you talk about fashion trends. The delight in your face when you make a new discovery. I appreciate that you enjoy my love of statistics. I love that you strive to be the best person you can be. I want to share and encourage you in every way I can. We've known each other just a short time but I don't want to lose out on any more precious time of not spending my life with you."

Just as Alex got down on one knee and pulled out a small jewelry box, his mother walked into the room with a sneer on her face and shouted, "What in the world do you think you're doing Alexander? You hardly know this woman. She knows nothing of what it takes to be a Davies-White. Or to be the wife of a high level executive. Don't go ruining your life over a holiday fling!"

Hearing her mother's shouts, Emma ran into the room with the others following behind her.

Alexander stood and reached out his free hand for Natalie to stand beside him. As he held her close, his nostrils flared. "Mummy, this is not a holiday fling. I love Natalie. She makes me happy. There's no one else I want to spend my life with but her."

Emma applauded Alexander's statement. "Congratulations, Alexander. I think that's a wonderful decision."

"A wonderful decision?" Her mother snorted. "Are you delusional, Emma?"

Sir William put his hand on Judith's shoulder. "You can't run your children's lives. Your son is an adult. He can make his own decisions for what's right for him. I wouldn't have hired him as my CFO if I didn't think he was capable of making important judgements. I've talked to both Natalie and Alexander. I can assure you that they care deeply for each other."

Geoffrey clutched his wife's hands. "Judith, darling, Alexander has already proven he's got a mind of his own by working with your brother, rather than the family business. Let him manage his own love life as well."

"Mummy, you've always said you wanted the best for me. That's Natalie. Please be happy for me."

"But you come from such different backgrounds."

"By working together, we already have a common goal. We'll grow together from there with love and God guiding us."

Judith sighed. "Are you really sure Alexander?"

Alexander grinned from ear to ear. "Without a doubt. But you interrupted Natalie response" Once again Alexander got down on one knee. He opened the jewelry box showing an emerald cut ruby ring surrounded by diamonds. "The ruby symbolizes my deep love for you. The diamonds represent the sparkle you add to my life. Would you honor me by becoming my wife and share our hopes and dreams together?"

Natalie's eyes welled with tears as her heart thumped. She stared at the others surrounding them who were smiling and nodding -- except for Judith. "Mrs. Davies-White, I've grown to love your son. I would never do anything to hurt him. I will do everything I can to be the best wife possible. Can you find it in your heart to give us a chance at love just like you and your husband have been blessed for all your years together?"

"I can see in your eyes that you love my son. And I want him to be happy. So yes, I'd like you to become a part of our family."

Natalie squeezed Alexander's hand and nodded repeatedly. "Yes, Alex I want to marry you and share our future together."

He slipped the ring on Natalie's finger. They wrapped their arms around each other and fell into a kiss that lit up her heart like the Christmas lights on a tree. Joy exploded inside her as she imagined many more decades of Christmases together. As everyone around them -- including Judith – cheered.

### # # #

*I hope you enjoyed reading this story. The story will continue with other books which feature more of Emma, Percy, Laura, and Cade.*

# AUTHOR BIO AND BOOK LIST

Christine Henderson's short stories, poems, and inspirational pieces have been published in regional and national magazines and numerous anthologies about family life. Her recipes have also won awards. Other published works include sweet romance novels, children's picture books, devotionals, and a cookbook. Discover all her books and details on new releases at: https://amzn.to/447yw09

Her blog features weekly interviews with best-selling authors who discuss their upcoming books and offer eBook giveaways. You can read it at https://thewritechris.blogspot.com/

*Thank you for taking the time to read this book. Would you do me a favor and leave a review on wherever you purchased the book? I would greatly appreciate it and this will help other readers discover this book.*

## Inspirational Romance Novels

**Christmas Moonlight Melodies:** *Music brought them together, but then fame tore them apart.* Nikki said goodbye to her hometown nestled in the Pocono mountains to skyrocket to music fame. She also left Michael, the man who she said was her forever love. It's seven years later, but she's never forgotten him. Now she's returning home for the Christmas holidays and hopes for a second chance at love.

Michael was devastated when Nikki left and poured his heart into writing songs about love gone wrong and gained music fame as well, but he's never stopped loving her.

This Christmas season reconnected them, but it's a shaky reunion. Their lifestyles and goals are at odds with each other. Can they find common ground to start a second chance at love or will they just become a love story gone wrong song?

**The Sweetest Delights in Life:** *Great first impressions can fall as fast as a souffle and become a recipe for disaster.*
Jasmine Cattrell has returned home to Falcon Creek, Texas after crashing and burning with her previous dream job as a marketing exec and a disastrous breakup in Los Angeles. Once again, she's working at her mom's bakery where she learned the joys of baking.

Trevor Lassitor, a food critic, can make or break businesses with his reviews. When he walks into the bakery, there's an immediate attraction between them, which intensifies as they share their interest in creating culinary delights. Only Trevor can't let personal feelings affect his reviews.

Incensed by his negative review, Jasmine angrily confronts him when they accidentally meet. Instead of blowing her off, Trevor finds a way to resolve their differences. As they grow closer, miscalculations and misunderstandings threaten to separate them for good. Will they destroy a chance for new love? Or will she find the sweetest delights in life with the man she loves?

**Picture Books for Families to Read Together**

**Praise and Play to Start the Day** This is a fun filled picture book that's perfect for children ages 3 to 8. The book combines playful rhymes of simple exercises and examples of praising God for everyday activities. The back of the book features creative coloring pages that focus on faith and giving thanks to God.

**A Special Digital Scrapbook Memory -** Eek! Who wants to do homework? Not Angie! She's too busy creating an online scrapbook about all the fun her family had at the beach this summer. Can't she just ignore her homework - especially memorizing her Bible verses for class. But a chat with her mom changes her perspective with happy results.

**Jesus Loves Me This Much! And Guess What? He loves you, too!** Through captivating illustrations and engaging storytelling, children will come to understand that Jesus's love is always with them, no matter what they do or where they go. Spark meaningful conversations about faith and love as you share this enchanting story with your little ones.

**'Twas the Day Before Christmas: 5-Star Reader's Favorite Rating** Go past the hustle and bustle of the holidays with a group of carolers whose singing spreads cheer and touches the hearts of those who listen. The tale is told in the poetic style of Clement Moore's writing, but this focus is on the first Christmas. You'll want to make reading this book a yearly tradition.

**Please Let Santa Fly! 5-Star Reader's Favorite Rating**
Santa's on the naughty list? That has to be a mistake! Santa is the essence of good. Could it be a push from those who are on the naughty list? You'll giggle and laugh at the funny antics around the North Pole. In the end, you'll be reminded of the importance of being good and kind.

## Devotionals

**The First Noel–Digging Deeper into Christ's Birth –**
*5-Star Reader's Favorite Rating*. This 25-day devotional and study guide for individuals and families includes bible verses, hymns, Biblical history notes, and discussion questions. Buy the book and support a cause. All royalties are being donated to a prison ministry that brings Bible teaching to prisoners..

**Exploring the Bible: Prayers, Poems, Praises, Bible Verses and Fun Pages – 5-Star Reader's Favorite Rating**. This book provides 15 lessons to engage the young reader. Each includes Bible verses to remember, poems, gratitude pages, and Bible related games, puzzles, & coloring pages.

**A Closer Walk with Jesus: 52-Week Prayer Journal for Women -** Transform your daily prayer life with this beautiful and inspiring women's prayer journal. Designed with the busy woman in mind, this 52-week journal provides a simple and organized way to deepen your relationship with God. Each week offers inspiring Bible verses, thoughtful prompts, space for reflection, and a guided section for writing out your thoughts.

## Cookbook

**Let's Share a Meal: Comfort Food For Family & Friends -** *5-star Reader's Favorite Rating.* Come join me on my food journey as I share favorite recipes I've made over the years as well as those shared with me from family and friends. Though I consider myself a "foodie," these recipe ingredients can be found in most markets. The directions don't require fancy kitchen tools to make.

www.ingramcontent.com/pod-product-compliance
Lightning Source LLC
Chambersburg PA
CBHW060748180626

46818CB00002B/498

* 9 7 9 8 9 9 8 6 1 5 0 1 6 *